Unmasking an Enigma

Roberto Meléndez

Unmasking an Enigma
©2024, Roberto Meléndez
Reviewed and corrected by Brenda Lizbeth San Miguel
Consultant: Rocio M. Garcia

ISBN-13: 978-1-63065-158-9

PUKIYARI PUBLISHERS
www.pukiyari.com

This story is dedicated to people fighting for a better world, more humane and less bloody.
To everyone who dreams that tomorrow will be more pleasant and friendlier than yesterday.

Synthesis

Laura tries to break away from a marriage mired in violence. She abandoned her life of luxuries and false appearances in Monterrey to return to her native Saltillo, hoping to achieve peace of mind for her and her daughter. However, her ex-husband (a policeman in active), continues to stalk her. In the midst of this tense situation, a homeless man appears in his way. Who is this strange reading buff? How is it possible that these ragged clothes hide a cultured, kind man? Gradually undermining her distrust, that gentleman of raisins will enter her life, giving her back the lost faith in men. With gallantry, the former stranger will light the candle of love in Laura, until she conquers not only herself, but her whole family. Meanwhile, from the shadows they are seen by eyes full of fury and longing for blood.

In this novel, Roberto Meléndez (Romel) presents a story, set in the city of Saltillo, Coahuila, **Unmasking an Enigma,** puts us face to face with the rebirth of love, with the healing of old wounds and with the firmness of the grudges. This story leads us to wonder, what else can withstand a broken heart, a broken body? How far will Romel take the torture of his characters? After what has happened in this plot, will it be possible, as he proposes, to achieve redemption?

With sincere crudeness, Romel spins a current story, in which, despite the advances of laws, violence against women and machismo, they remain in force. At the same time, the author flies the defense of chivalry, drawing a male character firm in his convictions and aware of his worth. Who are you? Brings us closer to the forgotten but still existing values of relationships between men and women, in a history of constant suffering, of doubts about ourselves.

CHAPTER I

When they got married it was an exemplary wedding.

Even now, after several years, people remember it. It was a social event; it appeared in the newspapers; it was announced on the radio. and on local television. It had an effect in one of the best venues in the city, an extraordinary event. However, the wealth with which it was carried out is not always a companion of happiness and today, like other days within the family, things were not going well.

Laura never remembers what happened before at this time, in the morning, that she would find herself so beaten, lying next to the railing in the hallway. She bleeds from the right side of her forehead, from her nose, and has a wound on one of her cheekbones. Her swollen mouth feels like a balloon about to burst. She notices it because when she opens it, to breathe, she senses the numbness of her lips. Almost deceased, she hears her daughter crying on the opposite side of the corridor. I'd like to go hug her, but she's not within reach, which she touches her arms to make sure they're not fractured. Her husband tips her one more beating. This time he's getting out of hand.

With oceanic eyes she hardly distinguishes her little girl, who weeps from the threshold of her room, witnessing with her innocence the shred of just two years between her parents, which does not cease for a while. Two furious opponents yelling and insulting each other, as fighters in the ring, in a disastrous spectacle, assaulting each other as if they were mortal enemies.

A few moments later, she fell back to the floor. She was punched in the middle of the jaw; a boxing chronicler would announce. That impact left her stunned, motionless. Just listen to his vociferous opponent scream, like Tarzan in the jungle. She feels him dragging her by the shoulders and throwing her under an armchair, as easy as if she were a kitchen rag. His broad corpulence allows him these maneuvers, his woman's body resembling a pen between his fingers. She makes a great effort and manages to balance her body by standing vertically, at which point she has his face at her fingertips and takes advantage to slap him on the cheek, with all the desire left. The slap resounds all over the house. She keeps trying to hurt him, with her nails, she assaults him by nailing them between his mouth and nose. Her rival staggers and twists in pain. He dodges her, but not quite, her nails, turned into claws, she reached her objective and rips the skin off his face, bleeding instantly. By mere instinct he takes his hands to his face and proves that the blood reaffirms his perception. This burns him in the depths of his ego. She marked his face. His paroxysm has reached the roof and now he wants to kill her, to avenge the affront.

As if it were a professional boxing session, he puts himself on guard and sends her three or four punches, which they hit frankly, without the least defense of the opponent. She revisits the floor and while laying, she receives a couple of kicks to the ribs. Pain forces her to bend; and be on the edge of blackout.

On the floor and overdue, she listens to his voice again. He yells stupidities without stopping. He says threats that sound like howls. She listens to a series of insults and humiliations repeatedly, that come in one ear and come out of the other. Now her punches hurt more, and she doesn't know whether it's prudent to keep defending herself or to let him keep hitting her. Her husband returns to the charge and tries to keep beating up his exhausted body at his feet. He tells her she's a cheap, sold-out fucking whore. Without respect for her role as a mother and has purposely neglected the image of a wife. The wife of a senior official like him, who everyone knows. "You'll pay for this humiliation."

"You and your alpha male figurations!" She replied furiously from the bled mosaic, white before, mopped with care.

From there, like a mole facing up, she looked at him like a thick wild vast, wanting to swallow her entirely.

"They're not figurations, they're assertions. Why were you so late? Why? Where were you? With whom? It was eleven-thirty, and Mariana was alone; and you were in the street, doing what?"

Instead of answering those series of questions, Laura preferred to defend herself by putting herself in the face of other testimonies, which seemed to be a greater weight than those that Oscar wielded ahead.

"And you? Why haven't you been home the last two nights? I'm asking you the same thing. Where were you? What were you doing? She refuted with a bloody mouth."

"I am a man, and I can walk wherever and at any time I want. That's why I take care of this house. I give you to swallow and live well. You don't need to be on the street. Let alone, at midnight, and alone."

"The lady who takes care of my baby left minutes before I arrived. So the child was only left alone for a small amount of time. And yes, you do support me, but that doesn't give you the right to enslave me at home, like human servitude. I went with my friends to talk, converse and hangout. Not like you, you're going out with your friends visiting the women on the street. Don't think I don't know!"

"With everything and that, I fulfill your needs!" he said, in a smudged manner.

"You treat me like a prostitute! And I am not!"

"Yes, yes, you are. But you're my whore, and I don't want you to be anyone else's. You're my property. Nothing else! Do you understand? You're here to do what I say. Period."

"Well, I won't be yours anymore! Go with your prostitute ladies so you can feel loved and be loved. You're trash to me. I won't let you keep using me, asshole! Go on, go with your dear hookers, only there you are able to feel fulfilled! You were born in shit and that's where you will come back to. And just so you know, you don't even satisfy me in bed anymore! Are you listening? You're not even good for that! Stupid fuck!"

Laura was shouting what was on her mind. Anything that came into mind. Without putting on the scale what she was actually saying. What she sought was to offend him, to assault him, with words, because this was her strongest weapon to defend herself. At that moment she understood at the speed of light, that sex is not only a matter of pleasure like sweet candy in the mouth, but it can also be a direct way to hurt another person in a very deep and definitive way. She did it on purpose.

"The one who's going to get the hell out is you! And I warn you, if you don't want to be mine anymore, then I'll disappear you from the map, you fucking whore," he stated with clarity. Screams were heard all over the building.

Arming herself with courage sentenced her out of her mind:

"I'm going to tell you something else, asshole! You're a street ordinary advocate. The king of lanterns. Street lantern and darkness of your house. You'll never have me again! Did you hear me? Never! Find yourself a street slut to satisfy you. It's over now."

To endure more was impossible for Oscar. He lashed out at her again. Like a savage, he tipped her a kick in the rear again, and again, as she crawled to evade the feet, until she was able to get up. From all the beating, she reached the bedroom door, on her knees she crawled quickly trying to isolate herself by going into her room, but he was after her to prevent any tricks. He kicked the door sternly, easily overcoming Laura's impulse, when she was trying to lock herself in. The mosaic received her again. Her puffy eyes stared at the legs of the King Size bed. Laura hauled her beaten body up to a five-drawer chest. To get up she helped herself with the handles, to climb a small hill, but made of wood. Next to this piece of furniture was a coat rack that hung her husband's umbrella from it. It was quite large. Luxuriously finished, it resembled a cane with an onyx handle, a rather heavy stone that gave the umbrella a greater body. She realized she had a weapon at her fingertips and was not going to miss out on the advantage. She grabbed it from the bottom as if she was holding a baseball bat in her hand, she made a launch that went directly to the humanity of Oscar. The hit from the umbrella immediately smashed his forehead, wreaking havoc on the spouse's haste. He was not able to avoid this one due to the proximity and surprise with which it was launched. While he recovered from the smack, she kept fanning for another stroke of luck.

Oscar, with everything and his height of more than six feet, suddenly lost the vision of what was happening. He went to the ground like a sack full of potatoes. His pearl-colored suit that he boasted about that day was turning into trash. He was feeling the tie suffocate him, he hadn't had time to even loosen it. He was bleeding from the cheeks and mouth from the first scratch, but now, wounded, it was happening from the opening between the eyebrow and the temple, as if the second blow of his opponent had intentionally sought that side of the face. The mirror would no longer treat him as his best friend.

Rabid as a spiked bull, he rammed her without hesitation. As if he were facing a street guy who was robbing him. He lunged at her, hitting her with the force of a wounded animal. On her face, on the nape of the neck, on her back, on the waist, kicking her everywhere, including between her legs. He acted like a robot, insensitive, totally irrational, out of all contexts of his reality as a husband, father, and man. Without thinking about what might happen if the blows to his wife went beyond the ordinary consequences. He screamed at her wildly, rabid, with a long-held grudge. With that characteristic momentum of a man who has no idea what he is doing when he is out of his mind, alienated. Outside of himself and entering an unknown territory where there is no understanding.

With everything and the brutal thrashing to which she was subjected, he felt defeated, humiliated. Heated by the gestures and revelations that Laura emitted. Her words had hurt him deep inside, more than the blows themselves. They were the greatest offense. No one was going to take away the right to feel the owner of this home, of his fatherhood and to exercise his power to govern the two women he owned at home. To be told by her that she was no longer his was inconceivable, something like stripping him from his manhood and putting him up as a scarecrow. So why would he have a wife at home? And then, you don't even please me in bed anymore! It was the last straw.

She would pay dearly.

Oscar kept poking her, even though she was no longer defending herself. Exposed, defeated, and crushed. The blows had been bloody and, in the end, certain. She was breathing hard through her mouth and nose. Her face was misshapen, swollen, drained of blood that flowed from all parts of her head.

Laura never stopped listening to her daughter crying now, from the living room. It was then when he, wronged in the depth of his pride and seeing the defeated bundle that he had on his feet, also, tired of throwing so many blows, grabbed Laura from her clothes, tearing them more, and with extreme brutality he lifted her up to the edge of the sofa with her body dangling, her face toward the cushions and the other half hanging in midair, towards him. She was totally defeated. She had no strength left to fight. It was exhausting to bear the torment. She was whimpering from the punches and kicks received from the aching stallion. Laura stopped defending herself. It was useless, she was never going to beat him. She even thought, "At any moment he will kill me."

Oscar, furious and victorious, without another word, pulled her skirt up above her waist, ripped off her panties violently, but with skill. He placed his wife's battered brown butt on the edge of the couch, He put his hands on the zipper and his penis appeared upright, to get in between the legs of the female, who could not defend herself from the harassment that was objectified. The humiliation hit rock bottom.

She had never been raped before.

In the trance, Oscar realized that he was enjoying the moment. Hitting and raping at the same time. It seemed incredible to him, and with all intention he delayed his ejaculation. Constantly going in and out of her body, watching her bleed was exciting to him. He was holding her by the long, tangled hair, he heard her crying out loud, he saw with lust her purplish, bruised skin. The sensation of having her hair pulled back resembled riding a wild mare at full gallop, the contortion in the neck was at its best. The scene gave him impressive pleasure. Laura was bleeding, crying, and complaining, while he had her strung around her waist. When he finished, he threw her on the floor. He bent down, grabbed her bruised face, and said:

"After I get back, I want hot soup."

Revenge had been charged. He felt compensated. With the account paid off. He put his gun between his legs. He finished his boldness and walked towards the exit of the house with the traces of the battle on his face but pleased by the way things ended. Confident that this time he had taught his wife a good lesson. Surely, she would not face him again. He thought that later when he returned home, she would be afraid of him, almost dread. And that was indeed what he was looking for. For her to have horrifying panic. With his actions, it had been more than demonstrated who the man of the house was and on whom the actions and decisions of the family weighed on. There weren't any more sufficient reasons to feel rewarded. Interpreting it like this, gave him the opportunity to assert, the woman in the kitchen and the man in the office.

It had to be that way!

After the affront, he opened the door to leave. Just then he realized that his daughter was following him with her teary eyes, from the back of the house. With a runny nose, her cheeks reddened and wet, she looked at him without understanding the reason for the screams and fuss between her parents. The warrior father stared his eyes at that doll figure. He knew very well that the girl was going to stop at that time, every moment that had been lived before. What she saw would never escape her. She would always have it in her mind. It would be impossible to erase it. Broken night, between his mom and dad.

He didn't say anything, he just looked at her, corresponding to the intuitive signal of his little girl that surely thought so much fuss had scared her. After all, he told himself, this beating had not been the only one. In fact, Marianita was already used to it. Still, he felt he had acted well, rebuking his partner.

***

After an hour and a fraction, the clock did its work, Laura recovered from her collapse. She felt the little hands of her little Mariana trying to open her eyes, wet, red, swollen, slightly closed, bulging and prominent. She pulled her to her chest, hugging her, although the intense pains in her body reminded her of the beating that her spouse put on her. She tried to sit up, but in the attempt, she fell face forward again, with the girl on her side. Mariana, drowning in prison from her mother's arms, complained bitterly. Her mother quickly helped and comforted her, stroking her as many times as possible, with her beaten hands. Laura remembered that she had visited the floor countless times during the beating. She seemed to have simulated the cynical attitude of a soccer player, those that drop at every moment as soon as they have physical contact with their rival.

At two years old, the girl still did not speak well, she was already saying enough words, but her vocabulary was still small. Although her tears and her eyes expressed all her lexicon. Laura, as she could, pushing harder, overcame the moment, and arrived at the bathroom with severe difficulties cleaning herself. Looking at herself in the mirror, she saw an astonishing deformity on her face. She was almost unrecognizable. The recommendations of her lawyer came through clearly. The lawyer had advised her that the next time her husband beat her, she should go to the Red Cross as she was, and from there to call him to plan the actions to bring against her attacker. She had not forgotten. Well, it was time to put her lawyer's instructions into practice. So, she washed her hands and proceeded.

The mirror never lies. And less this time. Laura was extremely abused. Whoever saw her would be shocked. Her clothes blatantly accused what she would declare before the Public Ministry. She grabbed the keys to her truck, picked up the first sweater she had in her hand, cell phone, and she held her daughter in her arms. She left her apartment with dozens of pains in her humanity. Laura could barely walk. She took the elevator and went down to the parking lot. She went to the garage. To get there, she still went down five steps and placed her daughter inside the truck. She had to clean her forehead and eyes two or three times, and although the blood was starting to dry between her eyebrows and scalp, it was hindering her vision. On her bruised arms she could feel the pangs still alive. She suffered when she would stretch them out, also when she would bend them. Her blabbing elbows revealed the scrapes extending to her forearms. She thought, "It was when he was kicking me, like a trash can."

She took her car out from the parking lot, stopping at the front door. She didn't have the automatic remote control to open it, so she asked the building guard to open the gate for her. When he opened it, the guard saw the lady in such a pitiful state that he immediately offered to help her, but she stopped him, arguing that she was going to a hospital for treatment.

"But what happened, ma'am?" "Did you fall? Did someone assault you? Just look at you! It's awful!" - Astonished, the guard chanted, putting his hands to his face in amazement and empathy with the situation of Laura.

"Nothing of that" She replied, denoting contempt. My husband and I quarreled, and I got the worst of it. See you later sir.

She started her truck with her little girl inside. Mariana stopped crying. The girl, seeing her mother who seemed calmer, settled the situation.

She was driving her vehicle going down through the Cumbers sector and going directly towards the City Center, but crossing the busiest avenues, she felt that she couldn't take it anymore. The pain in her arms did not allow her to continue maneuvering the steering wheel, and she intentionally placed her car next to a patrol car that was parked, without a driver. At three thirty in the morning the traffic was not intense, however, some cars were circulating, and some people were still wandering. She reloaded her aching humanity on the wheel and the horn began to sound without interruption, until the traffic policeman turned around, realizing that a woman leaning against the wheel of her truck seemed drunk, or something like that. He went to the window. He saw the bleeding and disfigured face of the driver, and he quickly called for reinforcements.

A few minutes later, his partners arrived. One of the officers offered to drive her car. While another patrol car drove ahead, they cleared the way between the cars to drive faster. They transferred her to the Red Cross at her request.

What happened to you, ma'am?" the uniformed asked as he drove her truck.

"My husband hit me!"

"But just look at how beaten you are?" Well, what a bastard your husband is ... eh? With all due respect, Madam.

"I know, but well. It's the last time!"

The previous comment had sounded like a sentence to serve.

On the way to the hospital, freed from the steering wheel, she contacted her lawyer through her cell phone and informed him with a rather distorted voice, by the evident deformation of her swollen lips, who had been beaten again by her husband and at that time, aided by the transit policeman, was on her way to the Red Cross. The lawyer in turn asked for details and other minutiae, but upon noticing that she spoke with great difficulty, he decided to go to the Red Cross and find her there. That was how he later came to take account of the facts. To take pictures and witness what Laura showed in the eyes of anyone who looked at her.

***

After eleven in the morning Laura left the clinic, patched, and confused, with bruises very visible on her face, still very distressed. Sleepless and depressed. Helped by the lawyer to take her home. They went to her house for one last time just to pack suitcases, pick up important papers, such as birth certificates, marriage certificates, proof of residency and more necessities like those. Of course, she needed those things. Photographs of her and her daughter, jewelry, memories that she still wanted to keep and the little things of value. After that, they escaped to her parents' house, in Saltillo, a city that is from Monterrey, they arrived in just sixty minutes.

The friendship between the lawyer and her had its good yesterdays. They had known each other for a long time. Since they were students of the Autonomous University of Coahuila. So, he decided to study Law, and she studied Philosophy and Letters. They held each other in high esteem. Nothing different was ever born between the two. A loving feeling between them that arose rebelliously, was never there. They had always been sincere friends. And they got there safe and sound, with on good terms. So, when they got to their parents' house, the belief and trust between all of them was unbreakable. They knew it, so they gave their full support to him to start the divorce proceedings. What had just happened was no wonder. Her elderly parents had already asked for it, but Laura had preferred to wait to see if things took a different turn, but it was never like that.

It was not going to cost the lawyer much effort since he had been engaged in litigation since he graduated. Litigation seduced him. He had several experiences in this regard. Since he was a student, he was attracted to that profile of Law. And all because, ever since he was a small boy, he watched the American films that later related to quite interesting legal journeys, he fulfilled his dreams of greatness. He wanted to be one of them! In fact, he had already won cases involving important and renowned people in the entity, of which he had succeeded.

"You know Juan Carlos," Laura said firmly, "if you require more information, talk to me." I don't want this to be misled. I don't want to go back to that bastard. He hit me like he was a beast of burden. I don't want to see him ever again in my life. You heard me? Today I place all my trust in you so that I can get divorced from that animal as soon as possible."

"Do not worry." "Everything is going to be fine", he replied, showing a lot of self-confidence, "this time we have him by the hair". There will be no escape. There is sufficient and compelling evidence for him to decline the divorce. He has no other way. And if not, I will threaten to publish his wrongdoing in the newspaper. You will see!

"You know he is the devil's advocate. With so many influences, he's like a wretched octopus. He knows a lot of people from the political environment, and he will do anything with his power to do his own thing. Imbecile!"

"Trust me, *Chiquita*. You will see that everything will turn out well. Consider yourself divorced."

She and her friend, the litigant, perfectly planned what they were going to say, where they had to go, and how to give credit to their divorce. The main purpose was to make Oscar panic. The idea was to fake it to expose him on television and the main newspapers, since he worked for an important political official within the government of Nuevo León.

After weeks, Laura and Juan Carlos met again and again. The lawyer kept her informed all the time, of the procedures, of the filed documents in the law offices, and of the court appointments. In short, they made a good team in everything they agreed. The divorce was successfully accomplished.

***

The marriage between Óscar and Laura had completed the seventh year. They got married in 2002 and were about to end in 2009, unfortunately things were going to end in an unexpected way, but there was no other way. By then, the situation was pressing. Monterrey showed the first signs of a busy and crowded November. A city of much movement and action. While they were married, they lived in the area of Cumbres, a sector that is difficult to access because it was towards the Miter Mountain in which people had to drive up in order to reach the destination. A well-populated area, with good people who can afford to pay for a house with a respectable, enviable quality of life, of a good socioeconomic level. From up there, you can see the city in its entirety. It had a beautiful view, worthy of the place. Everyone knew it as "the viewpoint" to see the breathtaking scenery.

Oscar had asked his wife not to work. He would always seek the how, but he would manage to cover the expenses of the house and what was necessary, as well as assigning her a credit card to make her purchases, without any mishap. The marriage worked well. Although he disappeared all day and they hardly saw each other during the week, except during their arrivals at midnight and departures very early, on Saturdays and Sundays, they seemed like a balanced couple and aware of their family situation.

Óscar liked to fix his disagreements with blows. Not only with his wife, but also with his relationships with friends. His habit was to fix everything in an imperative and autocratic way, with a rather explosive temperament. Of little social character, convulsive to the extreme. They had already accused him of having bipolar reactions, but he sent them to hell saying simply: its pure fucking envy!

With his wife things would go his way. He would flee and would leave her alone. He even left for days. He had gotten her used to not questioning him. Not to demand anything from him. It could be said that he did whatever he wanted.

However, when she would arrive home, Laura was interrogated as if she was a dangerous criminal. Where did you go? Who were you with? Who came? What happened in my absence? He wanted to know everything. Óscar told her that the inquiries were because he loved her, and when a man loves his wife, he must be hard on her and demonstrate jealousy, he would say, imperatively. At first, she said nothing, she got used to the way of being her husband. Sometimes with unhealthy jealousy, but other times, jealousy showed another sexual and benevolent facet, which comforted her because more often than usual they ended up having sex in a rough and harsh way, as he liked. He did not like the foreplay, nor the cuddles, he said: *A lo que te truje chencha.* Laura reciprocated silently but complacently at the erotic impulse of her loving husband.

Over the years he came to threaten her, arguing that if he found out about something that she had not told him, or if he came to know it by any means other than his word, she would have a very hard time, obtaining as Laura's response — not thinking of the consummation of the beater — holy and sign of where she had been and who she had dated. So, feeling sure of the reports she gave to him, she felt loved by her rough husband, who, according to him, rewarded her with exceptional sex.

Óscar, was very passionate in the field of intimacy. Putting ahead a challenging, cynical, and precocious language that made him feel master of what happened in bed. He exercised full control in every corner of his passions. Sexually, his manhood showed expansion with words taken from the street environment. Muttering vulgarities into her ear. Obviously, all of them, in the first person. A first-rate lover, yes. Possessive and obsessive, rude personality, deaf ears and without parentheses for feedback. No room for reflection. Without accepting criticism. Laura got used to giving, without receiving. He was the only smart one and the others were very stupid. This is how he described the society around him.

On several occasions Laura became somewhat forgiving of her husband's jealousy. By delivering samples of affection, he surprised her with gifts, flowers and suddenly, to her amazement, he would come home with impressive gifts, such as jewelry or watches of onerous character. Circumstances that were totally contradictory confused her. Sometimes she swore that she was the most loved woman in the world and other times, the most humiliated. Used by the one who flaunty swear to be her only man for life. Laura was never against him, she knew of his grotesque reactions and preferred to stay on the sidelines in that regard. Yes, but, in an oppressive marginality. Just as he appeared with gifts, she reciprocated with hot and ready food. A smile and her body ready for when he wanted to take her. So, the first five years passed, a bit stormy. Then things began to take on another nuance, which led them to events as mighty as rivers relentlessly overflowing.

***

After a few weeks, Juan Carlos, the lawyer, did his job. He effectively filed their divorce. He talked with some colleagues who had the same profession, in order to get advice, because the guy who was about to divorce was going to defend himself like a face-up cat: with everything. And yes, indeed, it happened. In the first instance, Óscar put forward a series of false assertions. Facts that did not happen that night when he boxed with his wife. He wanted to get away with it. But this time, not even with his influences, he came out ahead. Juan Carlos tied him up.

Despite everything, the lawyer had to endure two quite difficult confrontations with him. It was not easy to see him in the face. And, it was not forgotten, that the now sued, had invited him to his wedding. Furthermore, both had been students and classmates in the first semester of law school. In the same classroom. Today, the reason for their meeting contained other conditions, being quite rough. That is why things were not so easy to solve, with these mitigating factors.

At the beginning of the legal hostilities, the attitude of Oscar was overbearing, as Juan Carlos foresaw. The intention to frighten him to some extent was logical and obvious from the lawyer's perspective, but after the first pirouettes and pantomimes, things returned to the dialectical channel of events, and the protocol began to take the desired form for the Juan Carlos-Laura binomial. The complaining husband wanted to file a lawsuit for abandoning their home and for the misunderstanding from part of his spouse. But when Juan Carlos showed him photographs of her body and face, abused and mistreated by the blows he had tipped her, in addition to the written versions of the neighbors who saw her leave the house, and the part of the transit officers, as well as the medical analysis that she was subjected to the night she was tremendously beaten by her "sympathetic" spouse, she had to bend her hands and categorically accept the conditions imposed on her divorce. If he hadn´t accepted, Juan Carlos assured him that he would report to the offices of the local newspapers for having hit his wife savagely.

The panic of Oscar in the face of such a disjunction left him frozen. And although he madly loved Laura, in his own way, he had to give into the pressure of being in legal entanglements that exposed him to society. He was more afraid of losing his job and being exposed than facing a divorce mess. He had to stop from reaching the media at all costs. Everyone would find out about the damage done to his romantic partner. He had no choice but to accept the conditions Laura demanded to culminate in all this mess. Moreover, he was very surprised that she didn't want the house, or the car. Not even the furniture. That was the way he sensed that, he kept a gigantic hatred and clearly rejected, any attempt to return home, as Oscar argued for his defense. Laura didn´t want to keep anything that was the result of her marital imprisonment. The goodness of the divorce, if so considered, had allowed her to stay with her beloved Mariana, who she loved as part of her flesh. She wasn't going to let him take it off. And despite having prepared a whole legal defense with all the resources against him, they could not rip off the girl's parental authority, no matter how much the lawyer tried. They had to submit to comply with an indispensable protocol to the pre-established since the divorce agreement, where it was stipulated that he retained the right to see his daughter one weekend each month, in the understanding that they were together, on Saturday and Sunday. As long as he didn't go to the house for the girl. She didn't want to cross a word anymore with her ex. That's how decisive her decision was. The site designated to pick her up and deliver her every thirty days was the third courthouse of the family in the City of Saltillo. And so, it was. In addition to the above, Oscar was barred from visiting his little girl in his maternal home, strictly forbidding him from approaching his ex-wife to question her personally. Everything had to be in writing, by far, and if he had a complaint or suggestion about his daughter's education, he had to obtain that information from the law firms and consultants, according to the rules of this case.

After six months of coming and going, going up and down, things finally reached their goal. He kept his belongings, without his daughter, without his wife, only with his injured ego. And she stayed with her little girl, without inheritance and with the task of forgetting bitter times that did not leave her alone for many months. She did not even want to accept, even though her friend the lawyer told her, any money for support from the beating and abusive father.

She was reclusive at her parents' house, who were very understanding and let her daughter remake her life little by little, without haste, helping her, and providing her with all kinds of resources she needed to live with the family. Mainly with her granddaughter, who was so loved over time, treating her as if she were their own daughter. Laura's father was a retired man and received a worthy and sufficient pension monthly to support her family. There was no problem with that. Mariana started kindergarten at home and Laura picked her up every day as soon as it hit twelve o'clock on the clock. She gratefully accepted the help of the grandparents, so that they would drop her off at school in the mornings, while she went to work.

Time, as in all cases and in all people's lives, is unstoppable. Mariana spoke and asked, requested, and demanded life from her grandparents, and like these puppets were used for the affection of the girl who was like a blessing for the winter of their days. She dressed like a doll, spoke like a doll, was treated like a doll, and loved as a princess who is in pursuit of receiving the crown.

From her part, Laura, having taken five months' break, took a job in the offices of a publisher in the city's most credited newspaper. She began to serve as a cultural reporter. In time, she would become the Manager of that section. She rested on Saturdays from 2pm, after making sure the Sunday supplement was sufficiently prepared and corrected, to be published the next day. On Sundays, she dedicated it to her family. She'd go out with them to any museum, to the movies, to eat together in a restaurant of their craving.

Occasionally, they would go to sports city to eat among the steakhouses, their favorite pieces of meat. They put on the griddle juicy pieces of chicken or strips of beef, which they enjoyed in broad daylight, with music at full volume. And on some occasions, they went for a walk to the agitated Monterrey to witness some plays or visit a museum of their predilection.

CHAPTER II

The April afternoons in my Saltillo are warm, very bright. They have the characteristic of being unique. The shadows are left to come frank from the crown of the trees to look wide and heavy on the facades of the houses. When the sun does not find resistance in its way, the windows complain of the burning rays, which daring and insolent, invade the intimate territory of the lives that are transited in homes. Twilight meets, like every evening, in announcing the daily evening apparition. The drops from the slightly stained blue are felt in the air and the humidity drops from their sky, to tempt the flowers waiting for their dew at the natural coming of their everyday passage.

Spring had just started, and the horizon overshadows the games of imposing nature. The day is longer, the night is shorter. The lighting is seen longer on the faces of my city. And with that gratitude the tree grows and rises to the sky, the birds protect their young, the ducks in my lake's cross known distances without the tedium invading them despite traveling daily. And the mute moon is invoked from the guitar of the bohemian, which shows lucid with its white celestial thickness, spherical witness to the lovers of sweaty hands who take hold in the whispers of nightlife.

Thus, spring evenings faint and give their power to indefatigable nights. The dust, gases, and fumes that the air contained, surrender to rise in the path of the usual darkness, then, it is when the night arises mysterious after the invitation granted. One afternoon will never let you know in advance what the night of my city will do. The weary afternoon delivers my streets at dusk, always punctual. No preamble. Darkness makes with its gloom an indissoluble conundrum that only night can define.

The multiplied waves of darkness disguised in the shadows, monitor the perennial reflection of the crazy lights of high streetlamps colliding unfinished with each other. In that intermittent game it lends itself the shine from side to side. As the night walks in silence, in that blind space that falters with the firmness of the moon with clarity. The cool night fights the heat of the day and possesses spring drowning its burning between walls, streets, and plazas to revive at dawn. My city then beautifies. Declaims and sings, blooms, and grows, escorted under the influence of its light and dark colors. A holiday compass in which the climate becomes the roundness of pleasures, in joys, that are proudly given to the next day.

But in my city, not everything is sweet. In the distance and proximity, the ravages of the night less will be prickly, violating my streets with their stumbles. They use their time to vomit in the streets, a drunk man smashes a bottle on the sidewalk, another drunk man hits a woman for not preparing his favorite dish. Others, drugged, go to jail. There are those who are meeting others on the same night, in a noisy slum, they seal their encounter with splendid sex to make it unforgettable, enjoying their bodies as if it were the last night that our planet offered. There are also those who want to throw themselves off a bridge to end their existence, in denunciation because their street was not paved, nor illuminated within the aesthetic plans of the governor. but even like that, my city is beautiful. What worldly beauty has not been tainted before? Rome was set on fire. Japan was invaded by the atomic bomb. San Francisco succumbed from a deadly earthquake. And Mexico City died in 1985 in the face of an earthquake that demolished it. Even then my Saltillo will continue to live its nights with innocent pride, knowing that it will still write many, but many stories.

And just in that opacity of an April night in which the hours fall prey to the gloom, a man sitting quietly reads, leaning against a pillar. Beneath a mass of concrete. A gigantic road dealer pretends to be his partner. The man looks very gentle, he has a beard, sloppy face. His long, rebellious black hair is tied with a hair tie forming a ponytail, as women wear it. Dressed badly, but not in rags. His clothes are unstitched, but they're not ripped. He's wearing a black knitted cap, which does not cover his hair loss, but it's visible. His shoes are old and muddy, but with a full sole. The belt that holds his pants is as old as his existence, but he prevents them from falling off. His back carries a backpack that is not very bulky, it seems that he can handle it because he weighs it without regret. How weird! He is reading a book that is not thick, it looks like a pocketbook. It keeps him entertained. He seems to own his time and the space he occupies, that's why he's there, he likes to break hours into pieces. He has no calendar; if he knows it, it is not part of his interest. He is time rolling on the asphalt. A human rag lost in the ignorance of the city.

My city is his without belonging to him. What cynicism! He walks the streets without asking for my permission. He crawls across the pavement without being reprimanded by the police. He lies on cardboard and cardboard boxes regardless of the time. He has no inhibitions! He is not afraid of people. People are afraid of him. They repudiate his appearance, without even knowing who he is. He knows it and sometimes he abuses it. A man who does not boast of being one before others. A bum rolling on the sidewalks begging for alms. It is not seen that he suffers, but it causes pity. A pity that does not sensitize anyone. Today everyone lives witnessing begging without impairing their feelings. It is part of the urban landscape. A crack in the eyes. A humanitarian breath that has no sanity. In the 21st century there is no longer any capacity for surprise. They are all inanimate beings.

It's a weekday, but the bum doesn't know what that day is. He knows it because the traffic announces it, the noise, the movement, the number of cars rolling down the avenues. Anxious people walk, run, scream, roam, and fuss to reach their transport. Today is one of those days when everything moves, nothing is still. The air runs dirty with fumes and vapors. The sky that was blue illuminated while the sun visited it, is now inspired by the moon swaying proudly, on the mantle of its unwavering government. And heaven itself from above, watches the tramp enslave his gaze to the distant fragrance of his light. He has many nights of looking at her as if he is delving into her albumin appearance, he would like to solve the many questions from the interrogatories. This ragged being is as wise as the birds, which are guided by the sun and the stars reading their intensity and the geography of the sky.

The night has taken him prisoner. A moment when the tramp opens his mind to steal mysticism from darkness. And connected his soul to that triangle between night, moon, and world, he would like to reach an earthly experience that reaches the maximum degree of human bond, with the sacredness of his spirit. That's one reason for his reading, which he consumes with passion. He'd like to find answers to his everlasting quest and find out why he came to this planet. Why did God put him on this path? And also, why hasn't he taken it yet?

He's always under a bluff every night. Armed under the electric lightning. Sheltering in the solitude of his memories with a book in his hand. This guy's kind of weird. A street slacker who reads. When have you seen that! He makes no friends with other beggars, he rejects vulgarity. With that insolent attitude, it reminds me of a film released long ago in my city. They called it *Escuela de Vagabundos*. It premiered several decades ago, leaving time unalumed in the memoir of moviegoers. Someday my people enjoyed it on the big screen. The good news is that that movie has a happy ending. Looks like this *fulano* alluded to and humble, doesn't have it.

Suddenly the homeless man notices that a young woman got out of her car and moved her arms everywhere. Her car had a problem. He sensed it because a lot of steam came out of her vehicle's hood. She seemed to act like it was the end of the world and the monster in the movie seemed to devour her.

She has not been able to park her car properly, if she leaves it there, the transit agent will probably leave a violation in her pocket. If not, she will have to give hush money. So, she'll have to move the car as soon as she can. The woman, dressed in all white, tries to track someone down with her cell phone. The homeless notices that she dials one number and then dials another, and another. She certainly hasn't made contact with anyone because she hasn't given up on purpose. She looks at her watch once and then again. She is desperate because cars that pass through that side of the road distributor honks their horn insistently to move her car, but she's stuck with her cell phone. I don't know why today youth thinks God will appear on their cell phones and perform a miracle on them. She knows her car is the cause of the *chaos* on the avenue. Defeated, it's in the way. But she's still doing her thing. With just her cell phone and him, she's sure, she'll be saved.

She looks up, she looks here, and there, without seeing anything special. She notices the destitute bearded man leaning next to a column observing her, but goes unnoticed. He's nobody. He's a bearded lump. She walks two steps forward and two steps back, turns her body in several directions, without being in any place, raises her arms as imploring the gods of my city, for someone to have mercy on her.

The ragged individual stares at her. He's having fun with the situation. Moreover, it causes him hilarity to watch the brunette woman, dressed in white, unfold. She looks like an uncontrolled female android in the middle of many cars honking at her. He is about twenty steps away from the crazy woman, who persists in her attempt to ask for help, with her cell phone. The bum thinks that hardly anyone will help her in those conditions, since it's 8:30 o'clock at night, it's time for all husbands to come to dinner and watch TV with their children. And the most discreet ladies in their haste, they go home to continue with the female duties that they have inherited thanks to their prodigious motherhood. Those are the conjectures of the homeless man who continues to watch her carefully. I mean, the madwoman gets crazier, the traffic is crazy, and time cooperates with her madness. Crazy her, crazy weather and crazy drivers, everything is chaos in my city. That's crazy!

Within his contemplative analysis, the bum had a feeling of what was going to happen, that, if no one came to this woman's aid, misfortune will really arise. So, with all the parsimony of a colossal sloth, he lifted his ass by helping himself from the walls of his column that support him. And directs his insolent existence towards the young woman who seems to enter a state of total schizophrenia. When he gets to her side, he realizes she's out of her mind. She holds the cell phone as if it were a mixture partition about to be placed on another. I mean, she doesn't know what to do. She looks everywhere without determining anything, without compass in her gestures and manners, swings in the same place as if she danced a tango without company. It's eloquent that her stress keeps her knocked out. Look without looking and the eyes don't see who can save her.

"Miss, can I help you with your coffee maker?" The bum said, smiling directly at the face of the distraught woman, in an attitude that seems innocent.

"What do you mean, coffee maker? What's the matter with it? My car is not a coffee maker."

The offer seemed to her to be an insult before being considered a service. The truth is, her car was in the way of traffic for a while now.

"Miss," the homeless told her again. "If you don't move the car, you are going to get in trouble soon. If someone hits their car with someone else for dodging, they're going to hold you accountable."

"Can I help you move it?" He asked her again almost ordering it, but in a melodious voice.

Hearing the suggestion again issued by the foxy, she got to work, and she had no choice but to accept what the individual who had approached her said, but who was absolutely right. Her car was wreaking havoc in the midst of dozens of cars.

"If you'd be so kind as to help me. I'm going to thank you."

"Please get in the car and get behind the wheel, I'll push you."

"All right, I'll do it."

The homeless man ordered in a resounding voice, while pointing to his index the inside of the cockpit of her decomposed car.

"Put the lever on neutral, so you can move the car, please."

"Yes, I already did. Push!" She cried at the time. She let the man do his job.

Moving her car, until then, she realized that the stuck cars, a while back, started moving slowly and she was finally able to breathe more calmly. The ragged walked towards her without any concern on his face, gave her a smile and without exaggeration, very comfortably he said:

"That's better, miss. You see, all the cars are moving. You have already come out of her first problem, he said very slowly."

"Yes, but now I don't know what to do with my car. Suddenly it started smoking through the hood and the car didn't want to move anymore. Neither back nor forward. I feel like an imbecile. I don't know what to do."

She said while pointing to the front of the car. Within her nervousness she struggled to explain better. With her arms she tried to make his unexpected assistant understand the adventures of the case. Her dark, complicated, stiff face was seen in real trouble. She didn't know what to do with her broken car.

The ragged, smiling at her without a hurry, invited her kindly to open the hood, and to be able to take a look at the engine area. See if he could fix the fault by accusing her coffee maker, as he had stated. In doing so, he released his stare towards the eyes of the woman's dull, almost green eyes. He could even guess they were gray at any given time. The gloom prevented him from seeing the color of her eyes clearly. The same thing happened to him when he tried to identify the color of her skin when rummaging with his male auscultation, very brunette, dark, or perhaps black complexion, but bright, fading with the dim light of the lamp posts. Difficult at that time to determine the color and its texture. What he could see clearly was her neckline discreetly open, accompanying the fall of his half-wavy, disintegrated hair, around his bare shoulders.

"Miss, would you like to open the hood, if you'll excuse me. Let me see if it's within my power to fix the flaw in your car."

"Of course," she quickly replied, as she felt more relaxed and surprised that the "lord" wanted to help her.

She got into the cockpit, pulled the lever she located under the steering wheel and the hood jumped immediately. The man finished lifting the hood and bent over to search through hoses, tubes, irons and propellers, the fault that the engine presented, to fulfill his promise to see what was happening.

The woman got out of the car again. She stopped to look at him who now put his hand in her car, to examine it. His hair was long with a black ribbon, which looked like lace. A child's beanie revealing some hair draining through its broad forehead. He was wearing a brown jacket, ripped by his elbows and at the height of the closures, it was noticeable that time had done him his favors. His shoes, which were rather those mountaineering boots, worn and scraped, also light brown, but that with a polish would look like new, she thought. His medium-athletic body, of regular stature, did not far exceed her. The difference was minimal. Well, that night she was wearing high heels and that had to be considered. He also had a very bushy but not long black beard, sunken eyes, as if he had not slept for a long time. And the skin on his face was rather battered. Wrinkled, certainly from the exposure of the weather. Also showed acne and other defects above his cheeks.

This vigorous examination with her well-sharp senses was done that she ignored, what kind of man was intended to help her. She said to herself in hindsight: How well this man expresses himself, like a gentleman! He speaks very correctly. He addresses me with great decency. He doesn't look like a bum. On the contrary, he seems like a prepared person. She set her sights on the apparel and on his features. With his beard, it was difficult to see age, but she tried to calculate it. He wore denim pants, worn out with windows on his knees. He carried a wine-colored backpack, evidently deteriorating, on his back; by the way, he had slid it to the ground to maneuver better. At that moment she saw that in one of the pockets of the backpack, loomed the cover of a book, not bulky, but that she could read the title with difficulty, it advertised: "Rosario Castellanos" "Ciudad Real". Such a discovery put her at a real crossroads.

How could a homeless man like this bring a book in his backpack? Amazing? The finding was very intriguing. So, she snooped again more intensely on his persona and more scrupulously. This man had something that powerfully caught her eye. While the other, engrossed in his work, did not imagine what had aroused her curiosity. He was dipping his body into the front of the motor trying to find, as he said, the failure of her coffee maker.

She approached the hood of the car where her helpful tramp was in despair trying to figure out the seriousness of the problem. She in her eagerness as a researcher, noticed that he had long, filthy nails, but his hands perfectly denoted the manly drawing of his fingers, without a sign of extreme damages on the skin. I mean, he had big hands, but not like a mechanic, nor bricklayer's hands. He had hands unfit for rough work. That's when she heard him say with a little joy.

"That's it! Here's the fault, miss! Look at you."

He detached a hose from his position, taking it to her eyes to realize it was broken, with the ropes frayed.

"It happens, miss," he continued, quite calm and confident, "that this hose is no longer useful. It leaks and the clamp moved by the wobble of the carriage allows the pressure of the water to go to the radiator to escape. So we'll just have to replenish this part and put it back in. Don't be frightened, miss, it'll be easy to fix your cart."

"And what do I have to do?" She asked, to say the most.

"Well, go buy it!"

"Me?"

"Yes, you!"

"Where to?"

The proposal made it a very difficult undertaking.

"Here a few streets, there is an auto parts store that closes at precisely nine o'clock at night. Go and buy it quickly, because if you keep the hose in your hand, then you'll have to go to your little house by taxi. Go on, go!" He told her, while beckoning her with his arms in the direction that she needed to go to for the errand.

"What about my car? She said as if something were going to happen, while she was away."

"I'll take care of it, miss, don't worry. I'm not moving from here."

She had no choice but to obey. And after closing her coffee maker, in front of him, in an obvious sign of mistrust, she headed towards the stated goal, outraged because if anything bothered her, it was to obey the word of a man in any of his conditions. Since her divorce two and a half years ago, she had not obeyed a male order. It was a little strange to enter that realm again. But in no way, she had to walk in the direction the man had indicated to her and four, not three, as he said, were the streets she had to walk. But okay, it was already underway.

After acquiring the blissful hose, she returned to the stranded car on one of the breaks, which appeared to be meant to be a parking space in case of emergencies. In fact, when completing the construction of this huge road distributor, these concrete surfaces under the bridges were considered for such circumstances. So, the homeless, even in this, had been right. She had to accept it.

"Here's the hose, sir," she said demurely.

"What a good thing you found the auto parts store." For a moment I thought you were going to find it closed.

"Oh no! My God, I couldn't be so unlucky."

"Well, let me put the hose and the new clamp, you will see that your car will start without any difficulty." In the meantime - he again issued another order that seemed imperious to her - get a bucket of plenty of water. We will need it to drain it to the radiator, it lost it all. We must fill it again."

"And where do I get the bucket of water?" —She answered furious, worried, and annoyed because this damned bum ordered her as if he were her husband and she, his wife.

Yes, she had to get a bucket from a store. She had to ask the clerk to give her the cherished liquid and take it to where the homeless man was waiting for her, who did not rest in his attempt to start the car.

Until then, she realized that she did not even know the name of the man that was helping her, and it was almost going to be two hours from when the problem arose. But the truth is that this *fulano*, as she began to disguise him, helped push her car; in the end he found the fault that this one had; he kindly lent himself to her aid and had also treated her like a lady. With excellent manners. A gentleman. The downside of all this mess is that she had felt as if she were his servant. And that bothered her.

It took her a lot of work to get there with the bucket full of water. Pointed heels made it difficult for her to walk. She realized that he had already finished installing the hose and was just waiting for him to drain the contents to the radiator. He did so. He immediately ordered her again, but very cordially:

"Would you be so kind to start it up?" First step on the accelerator three times so that the gasoline reaches the carburetor again. Do what I tell you exactly! Please," he said, trying to be as condescending as possible, but at the same time to faithfully do what he was asking.

"I'm going there!" She replied with a grimace of bad taste.

She quickly entered the car, sat down, and hoping that everything would turn out well, tried to light it, respecting the instructions as he had indicated.

At the first time and in fury, the car responded by blowing a good amount of smoke through the muffler before the engine started to run. The woman leaned on the wheel, ready to cry, dejected, but glad that the problem had finally been remedied by a person she had never seen in her entire life.

Smiley but firm, she looked straight at him. He also gave her a matching smile. Without knowing why, they both held their gaze for long seconds, as if there was a communication without words. A reciprocal empathy unscheduled by their minds. They never conditioned the time, or the circumstances given until now, however, in some way, they had chemistry. Despite being opposite poles.

He approached very slowly. She cried quietly, softly, but she did not hide her tears, nor her joy. A strange oddness invaded their thoughts. Unknown to each other, they were unaware of who they were communicating with, but both clearly perceived their telepathic messages, rising above their gazes. How weird! This phenomenon had never happened to them. First time.

"Your coffee maker is ready, miss. I'm glad!"

"Yes," she accepted, pleased and undenied by the nickname adopted to her chariot. Thank you. Really, thank you very much. If you hadn't shown up, I don't know what would have become of my life at this time. I mean it."

"Simple to solve miss. The crane would have taken your cart and paid a good amount for the incident. In addition to the cost of repairing your coffee maker," he again dared to issue this qualifier waiting to break the ice for good."

And he did it. Laura laughed frankly and relaxed the situation.

"Thank you very much for all, sir. I really appreciate all your attention, really, you've taken me out of a gigantic problem. I would have gone crazy if you didn't help me in that moment." In saying this, she insisted:

"How much do I owe you? She said while trying to get in her car to hold on to her purse and look for a tip to give back that favor."

"How do you think I'm going to charge you, miss? I'm incapable! I couldn't do it. I helped, because you were in a hurry at that time and watched you look for someone on the cell phone. I guess you didn't find any friends to come and support you. I mean, you weren't fortunate enough to find anyone. Am I guessing correctly?"

"You're absolutely right again. I didn't find anyone. And just as I urgently needed any of my acquaintances, none of them appeared. That's life!"

"You see! How I am right," he said, asserting the comment.

"Anyway, I'd like to pay you. I can't let this stay, just like that. I have something to give back. Receive it as a kind of donation, please."

"Look, miss. How about you pay me with the book you have in the back seat of your cart? I realized it was there when you went for the spare parts."

When he said all this, she was stunned. Like a night statue. Impressed by the phrases of this prick who wanted to pay her with a book of literature. Oh, my God! Indeed, she was carrying a pocket novel from Elena Garro's authorship. A book she was reading, because in addition to liking this writer, to headline, she had presented a Literary Essay on the life and characteristics of her.

She couldn't take it anymore, now, or never, it was said. Leaving it for later would be impossible. This matter intrigued her about manners.

"Hey, who are you?"

Having said that, he was surprised by her question.

"I don't understand."

And he put for the first time all night, a face of, *what?*

"Yes, who are you? A man with all the clothing of a homeless man wandering the streets, who drives with an exquisite and fine vocabulary. It makes anyone think. If you want to pose as a tramp with these details, you will not achieve it, believe me, it's impossible. What are you trying to do?"

"Please forgive my daring. Forget it. I didn't mean to give you a hard time. I'm very sorry for my indiscretion. Excuse me, please. I'm going to leave."

He picked up his backpack from the floor of the banks of the sidewalk and threw it over his right shoulder, preparing to leave the scene. But she stood in front of him, showing no sign of revulsion for his appearance.

"No! She said it in an authoritarian way. Now I want you to tell me who are you? I'm not moving from here until you tell me what's behind this costume."

And she swept him from down up with disgrace and no complacency, so that he would realize that she needed to know who she was dealing with, so the homeless man had to open his mouth and say something.

"I am a nobody who rolls through the streets of this city."

She swept him back with his gaze, she approached him with no intention of violating him, but looking for the truth in his eyes, which were being avoided from her to confront her opponent's inquisitive eyes. She even came a long way to perceive his breath, which was not repulsed by her intentions to continue questioning him.

"Why? What happened to you? Why do you look like this? So...! Careless, ill-dressed, unbathed. Tell me the truth! Who are you? Why do you dress like that? I can't believe you are just a homeless man. When you speak it gives away your pronunciation, your good Spanish, and the way you express yourself. I'm sure you're not what you pretend to be."

In saying the above, she showed a new facet in her life. Something she'd lost. And now she was getting it back. Her female safety. She wasn't afraid of this man despite being the first time she saw him. She was trying to open up a stranger's consciousness. Open a strongbox where she didn't know what was going to come out. But she wanted to go all the way, behind this bum was more than just a masquerade of destitution. She was begging a man, who was all intriguing. A mystery to be solved. An unknown walk. A night owl who knew a lot of things. Besides knowing how to look at a woman. He had respect for his neighbor, sanity, patience. He knew how to smile. With a clean smile, could feel his mouth getting clean. She thought she was dealing with an authentic being. Today authenticity in a man is difficult to find, it is almost impossible. Usually, men pretend to be who they really aren't. Today's men talk about what they are not. They brag about what they aren't. They move in a constant simulation of the things they must live for. The truth doesn't exist, she knew it from college studying Plato, no one has ownership of the only truth, but this man seemed to have the truth hidden behind himself. She had to know who he was.

"Who are you? Tell me for once and I'll leave you alone."

"I am the hidden word," he said hoarsely and melancholy. A gift never given. An award no one won.

A man without a woman. A house without an owner. A dark night that can't even draw the moon. The lost kiss. The extinguished flame. The dish without food. I'm nobody, I'm empty.

Finally, he opened his mouth. He had gone many months without participating in a conversation. He talked a lot about himself, rehearsed it a thousand times walking in my city. He'd go to the Alameda downtown to compliment me. To surround the "Museum of the Desert" and sing poems to me. To walk down my Boulevard Carranza and would cover himself with my shadows. To know the industrial area of my Ramos Arizpe, without looking for employment. To sleep under the shade of my Arteaga trees and the freshness of their air. But this woman was opening it. She interrogated him to find out who he was and not to take him in custody to the command, as many of the patrolmen had tried in advance. He looked as if he were cornered. Tucked into a coffin with no hole to accommodate. He had spent a lot of time in vagrancy without crossing a word with anyone. Because no one dared to talk to a ragged. Countless months of being a certain nullity. Something like the indecent contemplation of a dumpster on the corner of an avenue.

He raised his face, wiped his gaze from the perceived obfuscation. She didn't reject him like the rest of the world. He felt her closeness as an aromatic perfume that awakens to any repressed smell. He had in front of him a compassionate and sweet face, who simply wanted to know the truth of his artifice, disguised as homeless.

"Where do you live, sir?"

"Here, on the street with the cockroaches and my friends the cobwebs. Columns are my shadow. And the shadows are my blankets. As a good thief I steal space from the city."

"Don't you have anyone to lookout for you?"

"I had it, but that someone left. I'm just a sigh in the desert. A little crooked mesquite branch by time. A plant without fruit.

"What's your name? At least that's what I want to know. I want to take your name tonight."

"What is the reason, miss? For what? I've fixed your car, go easy. Leave me here, I'm fine. You'll get home well. Surely yours are waiting for you." He said he was trying to deflect the infamous interrogation to which he was being subjected.

"Yes, they do expect me," she replied, not to leave aside the intention to steal the information she wanted from this gentleman."

"They're waiting for me! "She repeated."

"Look, sir," she added. You better tell me your name because if you don't, I'm going to start screaming that you want to kidnap me. So, tell me. Now I'm ordering you!"

And as a thing done on purpose, a police patrol was passing by just then down the avenue. Before answering him, he stared at her for long seconds and opened his mouth to say.

"My name is John."

"John what? "She wanted to know his last name."

"John and period, what about you?"

Hearing her utter a simple name, she thought she ripped this homeless man out of at least some of his intimacy. She felt she had gained ground in that regard. Although would his name actually be John? Anyway, she didn't want to harass him anymore and answered a little hesitantly, her real name.

"My name is Laura."

Just then they looked at each other as if a solidarity agreement had been born between them. Translating messages through the few seconds, setting fire to an existential plea. Handing out both notices and mass errands of good news.

Eventually she went to the cockpit of her car, took the book he had requested and gently handed it to him. He received it peacefully. He stroked the cover as if he had a fluffy rabbit between his fingers. He looked at the volume, saw the size of the letter, looked at the back cover and said gratefully.

"Thank you very much, miss, for your gift. I'm going to keep it."

"My name is Laura. I told you. And it's not a gift, it's a loan."

He looked her back into her eyes, and he found admiration in the glossy blur of her pupils. He right away thought. How beautiful is it for a woman to let him contemplate her! And let a man wrap all his masculinity. She told herself inside. This ribbed brunette is a beautiful piece that matches the night color of the streets.

"Yes Laura. Thank you very much for your... Loan."

"Just take it as a payment to your gratitude."

"Gratitude is a gift."

He put his hands in the pockets of his denim trousers, and the broad back was the last thing Laura perceived of the life of this person, which had left her completely anonymized. He got lost among the shadows of the concrete columns erected in the immense road distributor.

She drove all the way to her home completely ecstatic by the mysterious encounter with a homeless man who may had been Dorian Grey personified by Oscar Wilde, with no carnation on the lapel. She wouldn't forget tonight. It just wasn't to forget. She looked back and remembered. Her car broke down. Traffic was jammed because of her car. A homeless man who helps her. He repairs the car with portentous safety, at no cost. He treats her like he's a representative's wife. And besides, she finds the person more enigmatic than he thinks, he wears a disguise to go unnoticed. But to whom? Will he be a ruffian persecuted by law? A scoundrel sheltered under destitution. A drug dealer hiding in the shadows of the city? The perfect camouflage!

She came home pleased, satisfied, yes, but still intrigued and upset, that she had lived that unexpected night. Two and a half years ago, she had divorced and never later felt the need to approach a man like the one she had just met, just a few hours ago. A man who, in his appearance, had nothing to fall dead. And yet she'd give a lot of things to know him. What was the secret this man kept, so as not to want to be recognized by others? And even though he hadn't told her anything, she knew where to find him. If he had one of those impulsive moments that he then had.

***

This whole scenario reminded me of the unforgettable Walt Disney with his beautiful film "The Lady and the Tramp." Anyway, here and now, said the tramp got lost in the bowels of the night. That night that was lived in my city. A city that's not that old. It has its charms, is beautiful and quiet, and armed with history and people, which is good as the *tortilla in the griddle* and *the Adobe seasoning in the Jacales* of the plains.

I thank you night that you always arrive after the sun escapes. Because in your shadow my people sleep, rest, dream and make love. Or, like now, it awakens a mystery to be solved. I'll wait for you tomorrow at the same time, even if you're humid, I know that you will not fail because I need you to be, for you to exist in my space, for the blind to look at you, for the mute to sing you, for the disabled to touch you, for the sun to rise to you. For me to tell my city, that the moon is here again visiting, with the stars of companionship, so that she does not feel alone and kisses your gloom in the darkness from which she feeds. Come night! Come with us to sleep. Embrace us with your silence. Or invite us to the mystery of your things.

CHAPTER III

Nothing abnormal appeared in Laura's daily life after that encounter with the unexpected homeless. But this experience turned out to be a complete unknown when questioning it. Suddenly her brain ignited that memory, but only smiled when her mind installed it in her thoughts. She came and went from the office driving her car with respect to her routine. She resolved her affairs with ease, as always, fulfilling her tasks, attending to the requests of her immediate boss, condescending with the schedule of her trade. Things went well and others not so well, without stumbling in the front, clearing the normal rush of accumulated work, attending unscheduled emergencies. In short, the subject matter of her work commonly rolled, without explosions that would shoot something in the opposite direction. As a habit collected from her parents, on her desk she had within reach the portrait of her daughter in her school uniform. A small bouquet of flowers adorned her chest of drawers. Her phone, her computer and a couple of notebooks were where she normally wrote notes or orders to fulfill.

Sometimes she remembered John the tramp. With that caption she baptized it in her mind. Without intending to, she intercepted him in her space. He had left a good taste in her mouth. With some frequency she called him in her dreams, as if she was sleeping with him. Without being a nightmare. What would that man look like well-dressed? Why would he live in these conditions of abandonment and forgetfulness? Will he be persecuted for a crime? It was clear that it was not just any homeless mas. He was a guy with an education, prepared, of that, she was sure. His way of speaking was very distinguished, the way he looked at her, in a sweet way. A man with personality intrigued anyone, it was said every time his thoughts crossed her mind.

In those days and within the sentimental field, there was no busybody. She was very dedicated to her work since her divorce. She did not want to know about anything else. In fact, she avoided dating. On some occasions a brave man would show up, daring to show signs of conquering her, but Laura cunningly and quickly removed him from her hobby. She still carried the heavy sack behind her, two and a half years away from her divorce. The sustained experience with the animal with which she was married mutilated her masculine aspirations. "For me they are all the same." Nobody to choose from. Cut with the same knife. "*Patanes y machos*". "To live with another *fulano* who hits me." No thanks! So, I'm fine. No male to be jealous of others around me. She calmed down by counseling herself, better alone than with bad company. "Men are equal to gorillas". They just want to stomp us.

Despite the misogyny and conflict back then, she rooted a pronounced dislike from the words of a man. Reason why she rejected any approach. However, that damned destitute night owl returned to her head. She saw him with a candid and to a certain extent an honest halo. Seeming like a different person from the others. There was something about that character that brought her thoughts with his hidden personality. One morning she took a pen with blue ink and wrote his name with his adjective on a blank sheet, haunted by the intensity of that unknown emotion, like a seductive substance that circulated throughout her body, accompanied by a species of painful bliss.

She ventured certain nights to deliberately pass by the place where her car broke down. Looking for him stealthily at a prudent speed, without slowing down the pace of her vehicle, simply to see it from a distance, but she had had no luck. Then, already in the office, she regretted not being decisive and went directly to look for him. That is, without fear of finding him. Sooner than later, she summoned up her courage and went to look again, but this time, with the true desire to find him. So, it was up to the mess of the great road distributor, which broke the peripheral ring in two, where it was supposed to find him. It was half past eight at night when she arrived at the place, a time when, as he had said, the shadows of the columns sheltered it. She rolled her car over here, over there, down the side roads of the dealer, and nothing, she didn't see him. Incredibly, I am looking for him! If my father knew about this! He would hit me, for being stubborn and stupid. Not seeing him, she was forced to park right in the same place from that night, she was crazy about the failure of her coffee maker. Remembering that little word, she smiled.

Without despairing of not seeing him, she turned off the engine and got out of the car. She walked to the barred shoreline that divided the chasm into the overpass with the parking area. Her height was medium, it reached her waist. She even heard the belt as it hit the fence. There she leaned back, watching the rush of cars traveling fast toward the west of the city. Following the path, the end of the urban area was reached, heading towards the highway that led to Torreón. Her lost sight, without having a conscious gaze, peeked far above the fence. Cars of countless models buzzed with their lights on. The decibels gave her an account of the strident speed of the cars, while she drew that night when the tramp appeared miraculously in the dim light. She felt the cool of the gloom. It was about 60 degrees Fahrenheit approximately. She turned to the concrete column where, leaning against him, she was staring at him insanely. With her cell phone in hand. She smiled as she restored that image.

Tonight, she was wearing a white one-piece suit. Her waist was belted by a slim belt. She had a small bag, also white. She liked to dress like that, daily. She was a lady in love with white. She always used it. There were no different colors in her wardrobe. There was never a day in her work that she used a different color. In her dresses and pants, white was her favorite. Her dark brown skin fluted because it would shine in the light, it was the perfect combination for her presumed dress. In her office it was usual. She hated informality at her job, she was always very pretentious. The white was mainly overwhelming in her long clothes. She liked the one-piece dress, from the neckline to the knee. Or her pants with her blouse to be also white. Her shoes were also the same, open, or closed, of the same color. In her closet, white dominated her space. White bedspreads and sheets spread out on her mattress. A white life for a woman whose skin was very dark. The combination was ideal. White highlights her figure, acquiring a personality that, over time, became a benchmark in the company's image. Watch out! Here comes the woman in white.

She latched on to the only button on the jacket to close it. The cold was getting worse. The night did not look alone. The dark sky was wooed by black clouds with the impending warning of thunder and lightning in the sky. Will it rain? Hopefully it doesn't! She leaned against the fence to wait. Suddenly the closeness and human shadow of someone made her turn. There was the bum. The needy. Would it be okay to think of him like that?

She turned hastily to meet his gaze covered by glasses. Moment in which they gave each other an indiscreet smile of pleasure. As if they had both guessed the desire to see each other again. Laura looked at him for long moments, without speaking, as if to check his presence with the last time; Immune, strong, erect, bearded and with eyes similar to the angel of her predilections. They kept freezing their sight. They joined their intention holding their faces face to face, what a challenge to multiply. Competing the resistance of their gaze, to see who could endure the most without saying a word.

She relented first.

"Hello!", she said, unable to articulate anything else.

They did not take their eyes off their target. By then it was challenging. John moved to the fence in the parking lot where she had barely broken free. He kept the glasses in a tiny case that forced Laura to ask him...

"How necessary are they?"

"Indispensable to read!", he replied hoarsely.

He always sensed that she would return to visit him. He didn't know, he sensed it. Her eyes told him that night they said goodbye.

"How nice to see you again! How have you been?", John said, without letting go of her face that shone with the lights of the cars.

For Laura, hearing him speak again with that marked parsimony and clarity evoked characters from international cinema. Perhaps some resemblance to Clark Gable's in *Gone with the Wind.* Or Arturo de Cordova in his unforgettable movie; *The faceless man,* whose drama was rewarded by critics. She listened to him, as if he were a surgeon before the operation.

"I haven't forgotten since that night," she said bravely.

At the same time, she thought how stupid her statement was. *Who are you?* So that he would confess to me as if he were speaking with the parish priest of the church. But she didn't mind. She kept looking at his profile, his grown beard didn't look messy. It was taken care of, she noticed that there was care in the lines that limited his thickness. His black eyes glowed with the lights of the cars that did not end up passing. Then, without fear of exploration, she went straight to his gaze, but did not hold it for fear of being surprised. And in that swing, John's face was drawn among many colors that not even a rainbow could have figured.

"Laura! Tonight, you look beautiful, sophisticated. As if you were a nymph from Greek mythology". The moon suits her perfectly. The night covers her with such mystery that not even the gaze of a man like me, in love with women, can interpret the charm of her presence.

When he finished his brief, almost poetic qualifications, she wanted to hug him and tell him that she hadn't erased him since that night. That she had imagined him on her pillow as the man sent exclusively for her. An Ovid poet who understood what a woman's passionate love is. An Erick Fromm that perfectly defined the status of a love born feeling beaten by time. An envoy from Plato, whose philosophy was a treasure for the rising love of a lover. But she was puzzled.

She could barely add:

"I really appreciate your compliments but tell me." What have you done? Tell me about your life? Believe it or not, I'm interested. Have you kept reading? What do you read now?"

"A couple of days ago, I finished reading the book you lent me, Elena Garros', remember?"

Without giving her time to reply, he continued with his details:

"Now I read Rosario Castellanos. I love reading her way of poetizing her immense loneliness. She was a complaining woman. She constantly complained about the mistreatment of men. Look, this is a book of hers, it's called: *Poesia no eres tu.*"

When he extracted the book, he was referring to showing it from his backpack, the approach was such that she was fully aware of his height and build. She scrutinized his hands and shoulders with an eagle eye. And since he was not wearing a sweater, she appreciated the strength of his arms in all its magnitude.

From that moment on, they talked about books, literature, the vivid history of *Rosario Castellanos and Elena Garro* in the first instance. They agreed that both had been the starting point, the cornerstone in the struggle for Gender Equity and the National Women's Liberation Movement. Goals for which women fought so hard in the middle of the second part of the twentieth century. Laura began to defend the female precepts, emphasizing them with commendation, giving him a connotation beyond the ordinary. To her astonishment, John did not criticize them, on the contrary, he props them up, implying that he was aware of the inequality between men and women. And that dissatisfaction largely came from the education absorbed at home, with the parents. Corrupted inheritances of social roles, where feminism had been parked as an accessory for domestic use, should be leaked and discarded. They also chatted about the consequences of not putting reading into practice at home. That's what they were at when suddenly, Laura looked at her watch. Eleven o'clock at night. I'm leaving, she said in a hasten way before he made any comments. And without saying a word of warning, John lifted his backpack and pulled out the book she offered him the last time they saw each other. The book was intact. He had taken good care of it. As he took it, he took it to his lips and kissing it, he handed it to her.

"It's been a real pleasure to have something of yours in my hands! The tramp pronounced in a romantic tone."

"Hey," she said emphatically and confidently. Can I see you again? Although, I really wouldn't want to go back to this place to look for you."

John deeply admired this woman's bravery in asking him for a date for the future. He immediately raised his eyes upwards, seeing the heavenly journey of the black clouds as they moved with the complacent stillness of the moon. He took a step back. While all this was happening, she didn't take her eyes off above him. He smiled to let slip the hurtful sense of feeling trapped in the petition. He knew that next time she would interrogate him as if he were a strange man, but her body closeness, as well as her insistence, incited him. He was facing a brave and very beautiful woman, who wanted more than just an informal interview. This woman was not an ordinary woman, she was a lady who wisely intertwined the roughness of a man, with the delicate hand of a woman. To see her again was to return to the world of the living. John felt this situation was going to go a long way. And this was what he resisted for a long time. As he caviled inside, Laura crucified him with her eyes, as if he were a museum piece. At the end of many moments, he answered, very politely.

"You're absolutely right, there's too much noise here and too many eyes," he said, dampening the answer.

They both overturned on compliments each other. They planned to see each other that upcoming weekend at one of the many banks of the Alameda Central. Right in front of *La Escuela Normal* for Teachers. She asked him, as a requirement to the appointment, to bring him a verse from "La Castellanos". And he committed to her talking about the life of "Elena Garro", but from a literary, non-journalistic point of view. It meant that the next meeting was almost an academic confrontation. It was the perfect excuse to provoke the interest of a formal interview.

She was left with a thousand questions to ask him, but there would be a second time. She thought that the next appointment would be crucial, the important, the real one, the interview that would give the answer to all the questions she had kept in the trunk of impatience. However, there was something else she hoped to get out of this whole event. A journalistic encounter with these kinds of men who live in the middle of the street, could be shocking to publish in the publishing house where she worked. As An Art and Culture Section Manager she may well embed in the Sunday Supplement. Good idea. An article of this size was well worth supplementing the page. Her boss would gladly approve of a story like this, told from the voice of the protagonist. Therefore, she thought, somehow, she would gain some advantage from the mysterious presence of this cult stray.

The week passed when they both dealt with the superficial, the vague and banal. The days were consumed like candles at burials. The outrageous sun came out and went back in complying with its geographical round. The compromised moon arose and hid after every early morning, meaning time passed with a tight calendar, in which an unusual unraveling was fought.

She thought of him as much as he thought of her. And my city announced in its diaries the daily assaults, murders, missing, bloodied, the damn corruption, the infallible robberies, frauds, and dozens of kidnappings everywhere. Newspaper news that no longer takes sleep away. Unfortunately, the population gets used to the existence of the rotten, published to eight columns. Although ready to bring to life romantic dialogues like this where history does matter for the contemplation of good things, the same thing happens.

John had time not to live romantically with a woman. Much less about having sex. He came from a resounding failure that pushed him on unsuspected paths. But this was a female who already had him imprisoned in the same body. Brunette, very brunette. Of a cinnamon-colored skin that shone under the lighted lanterns at night. She had let herself be seen twice in the median darkness. Seeing her face, her eyes changed in hue and intensity, as if the lights of the cars on the road played with her sharpness. The homeless man wondered if those eyes would have any specific color during the day, because her gleam was not easy to forget. Those eyes were like literature to discover, like safety pins pinned, they were kept on his mind. She was a lady of excellent presence. He did not explain how it is that a portent of feminine and subtle personality, was concerned about a simple street bum, even if this one was peculiarly rare in his behavior. He was captivated by her ways of seeking answers, of rushing to know what he explained, a woman who wanted to learn by reading the mind of the one in front of her. Avid at knowledge, lucid, intelligent, with a keen sense of the things around her.

Meanwhile Laura had him printed on her pillowcase. The place John owned. His nights belonged to her. Though mature, he was a bold man, aware of what he was saying. She noticed it the first time. It's obvious to me, he thinks what he says and what he does. He's not one of those intuitive men using a made-up, improvised word. Having seen him again, she had intensified her desire to know what the true whereabouts of a man was hiding behind a disguise, bum, and living evil. Laura was sure he had a double personality. No one was taking it out of his head. She did not forget his ease of speech and safety when speaking, his aplomb, a crisp diction, and his voice particularly clear. That is very much his connection, assembling his heart with the brain, painting the exact arc of a constant verbal expression, with all its connotations. A man who, from hearing him speak, would make any woman fall in love with him. The appointment in the Alameda would be transcendental, not only to satisfy her curiosity, but for the pleasure of crumbling a man, different from others.

***

Laura had told her parents everything related to her adventure with John the Tramp. From beginning to end. They were going to accompany her that Sunday. It's five o'clock in the afternoon and John is sitting on a bench, reading, in one of the corridors of the huge garden that represents this city's Main Square. She sees him in the distance from her car, ready to meet him, not without leaving her daughter first with her grandparents, who inside, watched Laura walk towards the indicated man. They'll wait for her, they told her.

The weather is prodigious. It's not cold nor hot, but quite the opposite, who said something like that a long time ago? Maybe a Mexican President running around the masses? The Central Alameda in my Saltillo is very beautiful. It's been going on for many years. It's a bewitch for sensitive humans and a great lung for my city. It's my pride, I show it often. It has a profuse number of upright trees, a wooded landscape, thick, and nice. Its shadows are endless. There are pine and walnut trees everywhere and one or two trees of different variety, whose rebellious birth is visible. Among his runners walk the lovers chaining their promises, whispering their secrets. The old men visit to remember scenes from an accomplished yesterday. The students take advantage of it to escape, having a soft drink or enjoying an ice cream. Although also, in this place, business is done, or you get jobs on an agreed appointment. Perhaps, the closure or signature of a trade agreement. There are even tears rolled in a loneliness shattered under the veil of oblivion. A respite camps. A guard zone. A truce on the way. That's my Alameda, a pampered landscape.

He waits patiently; he has one cross legged on the other and reads a different book from the previous day. An essay by *Juan José Arreola*; that sophisticated writer who was wearing a glove and a pipe still in the 1970s. The sun has declined in the innocence of the afternoon, some rays strike the shadows and create ghosts in the corners of the wooded stems. John realizes that she's coming towards him. She's wearing a white skirt type A, her young legs peek a little above the knees, imposing at every step, well-formed, strong, and succulent, synchronizing a feminist swinging sweetening. She wears a blouse of the same color, but with tiny vivid reds on the sleeves leaving a discreet but ambitious neckline. Beneath it stands two well raised mountains ready to erupt. With shoes, white heels showing a thin small foot. She brings a long, wavy hairstyle falling over her semi-naked shoulders, which perfectly picks up the black waterfall. Very well combed. A face without exaggerated paint. Impeccable dark drawing of her features.

John instead was wearing his usual denim trousers, which he had worn for many afternoons. A dark long-sleeved shirt that makes him look thinner than expected. And a worker's boots whose deterioration is evident. It has been groomed a little to not look like a cave monster, not forgetting that the appointment is daytime and not at night. In the fountain has washed the face, to remove the deep dark circles from the persistent revealed ones. Chewing gum to avoid dead dog breath.

"Good afternoon!" He said, extremely impressed to see her.

Keeping her close and clear of the day, he fully appreciated her face. Gray eyes, extremely gray, like the clouds of a sky crisped in the face of a scavenged storm. Her eyes were two light bulbs. The contrast was wonderful, dazzling. The attraction at the time was blunt. She was a jet divinity dressed as a woman. Elegant, well-dressed, scented, with a smile as white as the garments that accompanied the perch. More than exciting him, he panicked to have a woman like this so close. From a very young boy, his father raised him to give his place to the woman, first in everything. Opening the door and giving them the way. Give them their seats. Take her and return her safely.

"Remember young man, he commanded him, your mother and sisters are first, you go last".

Weak sex are women, and we are their fellow helpers. That it, it caused a genuine grievance to man's prerogative. And with that in his file he grew, that's why now, seeing her caused his unease.

Laura reached out to greet him without any disgust at his street appearance. Instead, John felt like a cockroach next to her. But he was already there, so resigned he invited her to sit on the metal bench, where he had been waiting for her for a while. Each one in a corner of the bench. And they started talking about a little bit about everything.

They talked about my city and its characteristics. My people's crazy afternoons. Of so many cars that flood city traffic. From the streets of the city center. Of the countless museums that are on display and have become symbols for the history of Coahuila. Themes emerged such as the acerbated sexism of men and their eternal misogyny. Seeming to lie that in the 21st century they persisted with archaic and retrograde customs, which continue to be given towards women's society.

"What do you think of the Female Liberation?"

He was surprised that suddenly and without preamble, she talked to him informally. Laura sought in his enigmatic attitude definitions, concepts or arguments with which to sustain what he was going to say. At first it made him uncomfortable, then the situation went unnoticed.

"Reading Juan José Arreola who says, my voice is built by the word and she in turn by the memory, I find out about his ideas about the subject you refer to. Actually, I agree with him. For many it's a rough business, but I like the way Arreola undoes it. He says that the Female Liberation will be a fact when the woman ceases to be the one who serves the man. That is, she needs to define the sexual freedom that man has exercised unfairly for a long time. We have been unclean throughout history and forced it into submission, to keep its purity without its free will intervening. We need the *Universal Eva* to futurize its own libertarian acceptance, without submitting to the ideology of man. She needs to build herself and not just be the guest on the delicacy.

"Why do all men, as soon as they meet a woman, want to take her to bed? They behave like babies, everything they grab they want to take to their mouths. Why? I could passionately love a man without the need to hold him prisoner between my legs. Tell me, John, what do you think of me right now? In sex?"

"Wait, not so fast. I'm not a robot, nor a puppet, Ok! I'm a human being and I have my flaws. Please don't test me, you'll be disappointed. You are a very attractive woman, and I am not immune like the Apostle St. Paul to escape the carnal. However, I think that lovers come together physically because it is impossible to join souls. Lovers moan in the embrace because it hurts them not to be able to unite their souls. This was once said by a 17th-century poet whose name does not come to my mind, but I grant him reason. Besides, I've always carried inside that wise advice that my father sang every time: *love doesn't come through the vagina, it enters through the ear.* Now, I know that beautiful women like you have the capacity and cunning to seduce others. Seduction is one of the most powerful tools that a woman can arm herself with, it has such a dominant edge capable of penetrating the ice."

"Tell me something that has always intrigued me about men. When you love a woman, do you feel vulnerable? Why do you want to subdue her? I once had an unfortunate experience that marked my life. That's why I'm asking you."

"When a man loves with full sincerity and delivers everything. Soul, heart and life, as many say. He's afraid the woman's going to hurt him, manipulating him. As you have the key to our locks and lock us up as if we were your possession, then comes the bewilderment, the feeling of fury and modesty at any given moment. Those maneuvers undress and violate manhood, and that's when he learns that she already took over the situation."

"What does it mean to be a man, John?"

Laura knew that after the question comes the answer, yes, as in the Socratic majestic, but when you want to know the identity of someone, the bombing of questions is the best way. After all, she enjoyed hearing it. She had a feeling that this exchange would take her quite a long way. She recreated her ears taking note of his philosophy. This individual in front of her wasn't just any tramp. Could even be a teacher at a brilliant University. She wanted to make him talk more to be able to know better who he was.

"A man is nothing but his conscience of himself. If a man doesn't know what he's made of, he's nobody. A man is made to work because he collects knowledge from that. Work is the only activity that civilizes. And in turn, knowledge transforms work into reason that way a man thinks, because a man is a man, when he thinks. When you don't know what you are made for, that's when fear comes. The fear of ignorance, the fear of a real or imaginary danger, not to think about his ability to work."

"The man who is not employed is null. Human waste."

"Are you afraid now?"

The homeless man looked at her consciously, from her pedagogical, almost academic role, shown to this point. He thought, shouldn't be installed in that chair any longer. So, he came to his friendly and sexist side looking to defend himself about it.

"Every encounter between a man and a woman, prefigures the union. The above happens from the moment, both realize that after days, weeks, months or years, everything will be consummated. I mean, everything that starts, ends."

John tried to grab her right hand; she knew from the first moment that he was going to do it. She was permissive. He took her hand, caressed it, and kissed it, and then placed it again where they were, on her thighs.

"Now you tell me, Laura, what do you think of monogamy?"

She wasted no time in thinking what she was going to answer. And as if she had it filled in her thought, she quickly replied.

"You may think that I'm a little cruel, but on the male side there is no such instance. The woman is the fertilization of monogamy. It is an exclusive element of femininity, for that reason we have a different concept in terms of sex. It is obvious that any woman in love feels that it must be for her man, the possession of her sexual desires."

Just then she felt that the ideal question needed to be asked to address him as to his mysterious personality. The question she had had in mind since she met him.

"Tell me John, why do you live like this, in rags? What happened to you? I'd like you to tell me. I've lived the last few weeks with this nightmare. I'm intrigued by your life, the way you show it to others. I'm hurting your situation because talking to you, I know you're a man of good principles. I don't think you're a bad person. And I'm sure that underneath all this—she swept him with her look up and down—hidden another being. Are you hiding something or are you hiding from someone? Can you tell me? Please. I beg you to explain."

Now it was her who took his left hand. Muscular and large, veined and cramped. She wrapped it among her own, stroking it tenderly. However, he, with extreme care, walked away from his right hand, from that delicate prison and stood in front of the gray-eyed lady, beginning to detail the ravages of a preterit love passion, which came to the infamous desire to commit suicide in a hotel room in the city of Monterrey. He told her he tried to disappear from this world, but they wouldn't let him. He detailed his adversities and failures with Rosario. The woman who loved without limits. Always loved by him, and how it that she abandoned him by the side of the road is. A trap set, an obsession. He came to hate her as much as he had wanted her. Once sunk into depression, he had read *Las letanías de Satán* by the cursed poet *Baudelaire*, imploring his coming. Oh Satan, have mercy on my endless misery! To top it all off, he personally, at her request and in the absence of her father, had to go to the temple to deposit it in the hands of the groom, at the altar. Something inconceivable. What an insolence of life! In addition to letting ten years go overboard, waiting for Rosario uselessly, he was fired from his job for not being entirely efficient and often failing in his duties. Now after the time, he didn't want to know anything about Rosario and the only means he had in mind was to wander the streets and punish his pardon. Adding, "I'm a professional." I worked for many years in a reputable company as an Industrial Engineer, being Sales Manager for an important area. He told her that he graduated from Mexico City, that he knew how to speak two languages and had traveled all over the country. Including places in the United States such as Miami, New York, Boston, San Antonio and Kansas City.

Upon listening carefully, Laura acknowledged that she had found a man quite prepared and very sensitive, so she began to put together the puzzle. Despite this, she was not entirely pleased with that explanation. That said, she was amazed at the man she was dealing with. But she found it unbelievable that a person was punished that way for a failed love. Submit to an action of full masochism, simply because you have chosen wrong. Hearing him speak was a lesson in extreme exaltation of feelings and passions. But she wondered why escape her reality? Only by a loving failure was it valid to suppress yourself from civility? Something was unfinished, in the swamp of that story was there more at the bottom of his words? Sure. She wanted to find out. Searching for his soul wasn't going to be easy. It would be the purpose from this moment on. The question she would immediately be throwing was: Why didn't he work? Who or what was stopping him? In that cavitation she was there when she heard the horn of her car. Her parents beckoned from the window. Her little girl was crying.

She had to say goodbye despite her oversized interest in staying with John longer. It had been more than two hours since she left her old people waiting for her.

"I have to go."

"Yes, I know. But now I am the one who begs you and I ask you to see each other again. Is that all right with you next Saturday afternoon, right here? Would I like to listen to you and know how a beautiful woman like you is without a partner? Do you surround yourself with deaf and blind people who don't persecute you? Do you live in such a callous world?"

He put his hand in the backpack, extracted a piece of paper and added:

"Here's the poetry of Rosario Castellanos you commissioned from me. It's a cute, beautiful poem that speaks of how unspeakable a revelation can be. It's called precisely like that, Revelation. It is in the book you saw me reading the other night, I recommend the book."

"Is there a foreign book you haven't read that you'd like to have?"

"I'd like to read J.D. Salinger's *El guardián entre el centeno.*"

"Why?"

"When John Lennon's killer was interviewed, he said that book was an invitation to commit a crime. I'd like to know what it contains. And there's another one I'm very interested in reading, and I know I'll find it in bookstores."

"What's the name?"

"*Fahrenheit 45*", by Ray Bradbury. I've read its reviews, and everyone paints it as a revolutionary book. Imagine a fireman burning books and setting libraries on fire."

Laura smiled at the passion with which he referred the books and the pleasure with which he named them.

"Okay, I'll see you here next Saturday afternoon. Do me a favor, will you? Take care!"

Laura took the poem he gave her. Unexpectedly she approached his cheek and planted the farewell sound kiss. Laura's unexpected reaction at the last-minute left him to pieces. Shattered. He was stunned, and with his eyes out of his orbit by the kiss on his face, he shook her hand very hard, without hurting her, prolonging the moment of his contact, as if there was the continuity of his breathing in it.

CHAPTER IV

The heat of my city is not as hostile as in the rest of the state. The shadows soothe the spaces and the bodies come to their aid. The view finds the palm trees upright, proud, fully on its avenues. Slender they grow, eager to catch up with the star's height. The rose bushes are splendid and proud in any of its meadows and gardens. My people show them off because their greenish stems announce a flower open to the impending sun. It's a presumption for the eye, a natural color. The rose bushes of my city are the picture of choice in the usual photograph of my streets. A find of purity. My entity should be called the City of Roses. It would suit it!

My streets haven't stopped moving, some more than others, it's true, but at last they have the same instance. Quality of life. Whoever walks in them is seduced by time. Yesterday's geography did not preserve today's many neighborhoods. Its metamorphosis is felt, lived, and admired by the new forms of its presence. Except for treasures of architecture whose facades overlook the glimpse of tourist and small-town admiration. Jewels of time that are sustained aided by inheritance and its transcendence. Buildings confused between baroque and modernity. Between the nostalgic stubbornness of centuries ago and the perseverance of today, unsuspended with the designs of tomorrow. This is my landscape, cute and innocent, diaphanous and sophisticated, old, and new, green and blue, like the blue evoked of Rubén Darío that floods me; the aurora came later. The aurora smiled, with light on her forehead, like the shy young woman who opens the fence, and she was then surprised by certain curious, magical pupils. That is why today is the joy of yesterday's dreams and the living contemplation of a prosperous reality.

Déjame imaginar que no existe el pasado, a book says, and that the present of my city is a masquerade of time, which sensitizes the love hidden in my senses. History has painted it in its books. How nice it is to read a book and what you collect from it. It depresses me to know that the massive use of the computer and its inseparable internet combat it as if they want to disappear it. I don't want to be there when that happens! What will happen to libraries? They will show screens or cyber disks, there will be thousands of computers that will encapsulate the internet to inform the individual where they want to find them. The screen will reign over the lyrics, what a disgrace. I can't conceive of life without a book, but, well, that's going to happen someday, unfortunately. Everything will be shredded into a large capacity disc. Then having a coffee in a café will not be so interesting, there will not be a book in your display cases, there will only be information divorced from knowledge. I can't imagine a museum without books, school teaching without books. A university without books. Everything will be online. Will love be made online too? Well, to tell you the truth, a lot of lovers today declare their preferences online, so, I'm not far from that coming reality. We are entering a cloudy society set on the eclectic internet.

***

Time passes in fear, it is something that man will never manage to stop. That's nice. The promised weekend is here. The Mall Park looks green, warm, and splendid like every afternoon that love calls her. The love quotes name her, the minds ponder her, the light of the day brightens her up, and the phrases make her bow. This Saturday afternoon Laura is coming to the appointment right at my Alameda. She arrives on time as a watchmaker in search of the minute hand. She has painted her eyes; she has put on another white skirt. The best. She's done a hairstyle. The ideal. She's wearing a Russian-necked blouse, white with bright green, long-sleeved little ones. She tried it on five times before she gave her the yes. The day is fresh, she wears her outfit. Two rings, a bracelet, a discreet watch and an olive-green pin is her female weapon. It is ended by a scent whose perfume attracts the most difficult smell of the male jungle. It culminates with a shawl bought in Chiapas with a triangulated neck. For a change, very white.

It's been a while since she wanted to present her boss with a report of real journalistic value. Something outside the normal context of every Sunday in the weekly supplement, where the section in charge is dressed as poets, writers, the description of stories, essays and criticisms of literature or books of interest. But the opportunity to conduct an interview about a character like John the Tramp has never been presented. It would be very original. A being who lives on the street wandering around as a beggar dragging his personality to punish himself for making the mistake of having mis elected. Fernando Savater would have already lessoned the homeless man. Laura would get some photographs, a different biography. A moving story that will make an impact among readers. Something out of the ordinary to be considered, an outstanding note. That's why she carries a camera and a tape recorder this afternoon, which without packing shows in her hands. Even take advantage to take some random photos.

The clock announces, five o'clock, and he doesn't arrive. Her nervousness makes her warm and although it's not overwhelming it demands an ice cream. She feels her throat burn. Half an hour more and he still doesn't show up. Maybe she'll buy a soda to sweeten her palate. Six o'clock. Seven o'clock and he doesn't peek. The afternoon dies. He didn't make it! She wonders. When had she, in her life, waited so long for a man? Never. Never. And worse, for an unimportant wanderer. What was she doing in that place waiting for a man she knew of just his first-hand information? The whole week was watching for the Saturday to arrive, counting the days, to meet the infinity of answers he owed her. Why wait for him? Why think so much about this individual that she knew almost nothing about? What was it worth? John, to have her in this state of agoraphobia.

It was now eight-thirty at night. Although during the summer the days are longer, the sun is gone. It's been my turn to see the sunset at nine o'clock, it's divine and touching. I love my groves; they dress up at those hours. But well, Laura walks on the sidewalks of the huge garden with a lost look at the lush trees that fade at that hour. It is high on the sidewalk and from the corner comes the tone of an old melody, very old, of a Brazilian dwarf singer, which we all met once as Nelson Ned...

Who are you?
you suddenly appeared in my life
reviving the lost illusion
who long ago slept inside me.

Right, she said, I only know his name. What did I feel about this man? What absurd feeling is awakened by someone you don't know? Even if that someone was obviously different, incomparable, exceptional. A commoner! Someone who has the exact words on his lips, someone whose conversation gives meaning to any mind in mid-flight. He was someone she didn't know, but she suffered from his absence. It wasn't the only time she liked a man, but it was the first one a man would sensitize her estrogen production. She'd have to admit it. Moreover, the perception of euphoria caused her by his closeness was undeniable. She surfaced in a second, the puerile excitement of a preparatory school just as the groom dares with the initial babbling. She got in the car. She still managed to drive with the song musicalizing inside. *Who are you? That you suddenly appeared in my life to have me in these stupid conditions.*

It was dark in the nascent tremor of her desires. Hot and embarrassing night. The humidity always added to the heat, provides a feeling of unbearable discomfort. The lights of the cars heralded the darkness. Laura didn't turn on the radio. For what? She was driving with her silence in tow, as heavy as the world she lived in. Why didn't he come? Why did he miss the appointment? Would something had happened to you? But he's a bum! A stray who may have lied and you fell into the hole. But why? I see the way he looks at me, he's attracted to me, I know! Did the mirror tell you that you own his feelings? Who are you? To feel like his owner. What did I tell him that hurt him? Where do I look for him? In the same place? When should I look for him again? But he's a Nobody! Why am I crying? Because of him? Or because I'm lonely. Why?

She fell into the tunnel of despondent. Laura stood like the lifeline of a penitent who seeks forgiveness for her sin. She sarcastically underlined her failed intention. She had thought she had an important news story to publish in the paper and take advantage of an enigmatic encounter. An intelligent poet bum golfing in our city. Get to know him! An exemplary being, a diamond in the rough in search of inner peace. Bah! It turned out to be her, the prey she had cornered. How to publish something that didn't end? It had wasteful information, very simple. Starting because of the famous John, she had no full name of. No age, no whereabouts. He had told an incredibly romantic, exaggerated story that did not tie with reality.

***

It happened one night, while at home, her father heard her sobbing behind her bedroom door. He knocked before entering. Slowly, he entered the room after the permission. He approached her slowly, with that paternal tenderness, that maturity announces when love exists. He was an old worshipper of his daughter and granddaughter. He would give anything for them, so was life itself.

"What's the matter, daughter?"

"I don't want to tell you anything, I'm embarrassed!"

"What shame can there be among us? I'm your father and you're my daughter. Come on tell me, what's the matter with you? Cry calmly, cast out that sadness. Put your head on my chest and let me hold you. Don't be afraid, tell me. I want to listen to you, see if I can give you advice or something to help you. Go! Be good.

Laura seized the moment and told her father about her sorrows. She told him she was lonely and depressed. The image of that tramp had made her feel abandoned. "I was thinking too much about him". Am I making a mistake father, thinking about a street bum? She had something that imprisoned her brain and oppressed her heart in an inconceivable way.

Surprised she was of herself, absorbed, with the *quijotesca* figure of a stranger in mind. How does God allow a hatful to have me in these pitiful conditions? How is it possible that having more than six billion humans on the planet, I am infatuated with a homeless fool?

"I am afraid of confusing the compassion or pity of a street individual, with the desire arising from a sentimental whim."

"Don't forget that God is not only in the Bible, but he is also standing by your window, at the table, and right now he is sleeping on your bed."

Her old man told her what he could, what he found in the trunk of his experience.

"I'll always tell you, my daughter. Neither evil nor good are statistics, they are only an instant in our lives, then they go elsewhere, to take care of other people, from another city and another house that is not ours." He kissed her forehead, laid it down and witnessed her rest on the pillow, only then did he leave her room with good wishes for his daughter.

Many days without hearing from him were like the hangover after a drunken night. Something dreadful, with her throat about to burst. Her gastritis caused crises during office hours, burning inside the esophagus. Her mouth vomited violence, accusing an angry temper. She would arrive very early, and she was leaving very late, intentionally. She didn't want to be alone with herself. Who paid for the broken dishes were her collaborators who ignored why she was so irritable and exasperated. The white looked dark. With a prepotent, insulting, derogatory, and inaccessible attitude to rip away from her any satisfaction. She would not eat most of the time. Sometimes she would run out of food. She would swallow little things, a sandwich, a fruit or a cookie, and the days rolled by like taxis in a city. Endless days and nights with no truce or peace. Her parents, who knew the origins of the situation thought this reaction was merely transient and took it calmly and patiently.

She couldn't forget him. He was stuck in her mind as if it were an extraordinary test. An unpayable debt that would corner her into immerse thinking on how to get rid of the problem. There were sometimes when innocently imagined that he would go looking for her, but how, if she never told him about her whereabouts. Not at home or in the office. She thought she saw him wandering the streets around. Even on a couple of occasions she went looking for him under the bridge, at the intersections, like the last time, but without fortune. She didn't find him.

The inexorable running of the weeks began to do its thing, to relieve, but not to heal the wound. Countless hard-working afternoons passed. Conducting interviews, writing, pending columns, essays, stories, correcting, editing, supervising. At the same time, she also took care of her daughter Mariana and her crazy antics. To love her parents, to seek them, to be with them, to talk to them about her things, and to entrust them with some secrets. After three months she managed to make things slowly distended. The anxiety of that bad afternoon at the mall lasted the entire fall season. Dreaming was nothing serious when hope was consolidated. But she didn't even have that. From John, she had only kept his word.

***

While John, the homeless man was gradually leaving her mind, Oscar, Mariana's father, kept her uneasy. More often than sometimes he violated the rules imposed by the judge. Suddenly in the mornings when she left home, she saw him inside his car. Parked in the corner. In an attitude of close vigilance. Always alone at the front of the wheel. Without taking his eyes off her and watching her, simply seeing what she was carrying in her hands. As she drove to her office, Oscar went behind without obstructing her path, without trying to stop her. He was after her as if his car were an object of espionage in the time of the Cold War. Upon entering the parking lot of the building where she worked, he got lost in the surrounding streets without any fuss. The same thing happened other times, while Laura was traveling with her parents and daughter. She watched him through the rearview mirror, noticing his insistence. It was an insane persecution that did not come any further, because he did not intervene in anything with her family. A cynical and bold belligerent act. He just spied, watched, and never minded being seen by her. The family turned around, going in the back of the car cab to corroborate his intransigence. I can't explain it, Laura commented, how he comes here from Monterrey in the mornings, just to annoy us with his stupid behavior.

Nearly three years had passed, and her ex-husband persisted with such maneuvers, strange and mysterious behaviors. It seemed that Oscar was interested in being seen by Laura and her family. He wanted to scare her through that strange surveillance. He did it often, intentionally. The end enclosed the intention to probably do something that would later be put into practice, but for now it was enough to make himself present. He was chasing her without telling her anything or hurting her. He wanted to cause her unease and make Laura think that she wasn't free. To put into her thinking that she was still a divorced prisoner of Oscar. From his ex-partner, who was still considered to be his owner. His possessiveness had not culminated in marital separation. He wanted to prove to her that she was still his. That she belonged to him. And that's how he wanted her to play it. He wanted to subdue her like a sheep at the zoo.

Oscar was an irascible man, with a sour temper. Very determined to give prompt purpose to his objectives. Practical in what he wanted for his particular life. What he considered his, no one took it from him, fought like a wolf for his prey. A one-word guy, that is, what he thought or said was what had to be done, there was no other. He was fine and the others were assholes. His propositions were almost military mandates. They had to be done just as he had ordered them. Just as he obeyed his superiors, blindly, he liked to be obeyed the same way, without any questions. A valuable virtue in which his superiors would cultivate his reliability, a confident and loyal man, applied to his work. He complied with the orders issued by his superior accurately and in time. Nevertheless, he was considered an effective man.

This behavioral trajectory would constantly manifest her. Thus, he was known in the middle where he exhibited. A cold, cabal, straight, strict, discreet guy and most importantly for his bosses; a non-questioner. Like a robot, he took orders and executed them. That's why in his marital life he demanded to be treated like a man of courage. He had a boss whom he respected and revered. Similarly, he wanted his partner to commend, reward and please him as if he were a God at the height of paradise. He didn't care that he wasn't the best for Laura, he wanted everything from his spouse, submission, and surrender, if possible, her existence. Feeling rewarded for what he brought home was essential. He demanded a clean house, a good dish on the table, his clothes washed, ironed, ready to wear, without his wife forgetting of course, to please him with an affable, gentle, smiling face that made him feel in a home where he was the most important piece of family chess. Boasting himself that without his virile contribution Laura would not have had her Mariana. Without him, she wouldn't have conceived her. It was clear! However, to his misfortune he thought, she had not thanked him.

He studied law at the Autonomous University of Coahuila campus Saltillo. He had a clean transcript, without any failing subjects and titling himself with an average that exceeded a ninety average. Always neat, very serious, he was not known for great friendships, antisocial, young with few words, but very applied to his studies. His teachers had no complaints about his performance both outside and inside the classroom. Always well presented, fulfilling his homework and classwork that would put entrust to him. Through the bank he received money from his father for his support. He would send it to him from *Piedras Negras*. His classmates thought they sent him more than enough, because he was driving a newly modeled car. He wasn't a student who smiled. He would rarely share, very isolated, and away from classmates. Respectful to every person. That's how he wanted to be treated. When someone overjoyed himself with some joke or foul comment that affected him, he immediately put in his place the one who had slipped the taunt. He would make a quick argument: *I don't mess with anyone, so don't mess with me.*

He won Laura's heart the good way and with his good intentions. He would bring her flowers once in a while. He would invite her to the movies without surpassing himself. When the time came, he took her home. He always bragged to his friends. First her and then him. He would buy her what was within his reach and almost always had the courage in his present, so that Laura would feel truly grateful. Anyway, a man with a full beard. Oscar was an irreversible guy. Once an order was issued, it had to be executed. If he fulfilled all the duties of a parent and husband, then Laura should give her passions in return. She had to be there for him the same way he wanted to be. She had to settle for what Oscar gave her, what he put on her, what he offered her and even in matters of love there was no possibility of rejection. To do so was to predict an earthquake of great consequences. She had to wait for him at home all day. Every time he came, she would feed him and serve him like the lord. When he went to bed, she had to go back without laughing. Laura was also subject to ask permission to go out to see her friends. To visit her parents. To buy her little girl a piece of clothing. She had to tell him when she went out to fill the pantry and when something strange or unusual would happen in her family life.

When the instructions were not fully complied with, his reactions were violent. He would scream, scaring the little girl. He would start by pushing Laura as his first ape interventions. Then the complaints and discussions would rise in tone and then the slaps would make their appearance. He soon became a gorilla and ended up being a monster to the family. Until we came to the end that we already knew.

Even though the years passed like water in the river, Oscar still held a great grudge. He would not assimilate his separation. He was hurt on the way she left home. She never did it before. That's why he didn't think she'd dare. In addition, Mariana was ripped from him, despised the belongings that he had bought her, she threatened him with a lawyer to report the abuse to which she was subjected while living with him. In short, he came out with his tail between his legs. And that hurt him. Still today he kept showing among his fingers the wedding ring. Within his deep wound, marked by his ex-wife's indifference, it was said many times that as long as he was not happy with another woman, it would prevent Laura from being happy with another man. Pain with pain must be paid, he assured.

He didn't have a sentimental life. The brothels after a drink were his fondness. With his money he obtained for a while a woman like the ones of the beginning of the century, subdued, subjected, selfless, quiet, conforming, and loving. He knew it was hard to come across such a specimen, like the one he once had at home.

***

Instead, with Laura's new life, the present or future of who her husband was, was not given a damn. She had turned the page, as they say. Delete and new account. If he was hanging out with one or was with another. She didn't even notice. If he was married. If he kept his job or bought a new car. It was none of her business. Laura was doing everything for her life and her loved ones. She lived with her parents, was dedicated to her work, to the education of her little girl and to the events that arose from there, making her live as before. Happy. Other than that, she let the world rotate. Nothing mattered to her, absolutely nothing, much less the life of who her spouse was. If she didn't know anything about him, it was better for her. Her ex-husband's physical and moral integrity was a zero to the left. She just hoped that under the sexist stigma this would not frustrate her the day she wanted to engage emotionally with someone else. Almost three years of not being with that troglodyte was a gift of peace that she now enjoyed.

Since her marriage separation, no one had come close to her. Why think about sex if she didn't have someone to do it with? She thought the same as Don Facundo Cabral when he said: *"So why be hungry if I don't have to eat." To make and have sex you have to feel love for a partner.* And to find a partner; having started a relationship, old roots of her parents, wanting it to fulfill despite being in the 21st century. Ordinarily she lived with her obligations, without love at the door. Indeed however, with many barking at her behind, but without having anyone take her sleep away. They were all the same. She saw the same face as her ex-husband. Maybe that's why John attracted her so much because she was looking at his intellect. An individual with a different episode. An exceptional life. A perfect semiotics to make the signs of her path more bearable. A metaphor wandering around to respond to the leaks of the mind, in desperation of knowing where you are today and what you will do tomorrow.

Then she couldn't sleep. Nights were as long as the deserts on the planet Mars. Drawing monsters in her mind, devouring their dreams. Gliding through anxiety in search of comfort. It wasn't possible to live like this. *"I can't isolate myself from what I need to live."* I'd like to be someone's. Feeling like someone's owner. Perceive the harmonious assurance of being in the thought of the one who loves you and needs you. Have a reason to live every morning. I don't want to run abroad like *"La Castellanos"* for not feeling loved. I also don't want to be as irreverent as *"La Garro"* reneging on my luck for the days I get to live. At my thirty-four, I can still afford to choose before I'm chosen.

A few months later, reading the paper in the show section, she noticed some titles that caught her eye. The play "A Solid Home" was announced precisely by the writer *Elena Garro*. The play will be performed in a theater in the city of Monterrey. She bought the tickets online and told her parents to be on the lookout for the show, she bought tickets for everyone. The date didn't make her beg; it was quick. They took the road and, in an hour, punctual, they were like good fans of the theater, waiting for the play of the season to begin. Although the theater was not crowded, in fact, it featured rows to be filled, Laura realized that attendance was more or less regular.

She was very interested in seeing this play. It usually came in three parts. And she felt morbid to know how they were going to stage it. Laura kept this writer's novels in her library. She was a lover of his career as such. Thus, knowing of its content, she wanted to witness it and find the differences between the written and the acting. Rarely was this play performed in any theater in the country.

She would turn back and forth without giving importance to anything in particular. Although there was a time when she found eyes that seemed familiar to her. The neighborhood of many people sitting and standing in the theater room did not let her clarify her vision. However, between the rows of the seats and the people going up and down, she recognized a face that was distinguished from others. He looked familiar. Something in the profile of that man evoked a persistent memory. Manly and vigorous. Attractive. Those boys whose personality makes any woman turn.

She disguised him with those eyes that disturbed her, even made her impatient. It looks like he found her first, because he didn't take his eyes off her either. A bearded and caring face, with short hair, well groomed. Piercing eyes are like a drill that reaches the consciousness of the one who looks at them. A face you don't forget. It penetrates the marrow. That he has life in another life. At first, she looked at him in disguise, but then it became impossible to not look at him anymore. The strange thing was that this man, also looked at her without any modesty, and the intensity of his inspection towards her turning to look for him irretrievably, leaning over her eyes. And so it was, until he rose from his seat with all the desire to let himself be seen, and blatantly entered the visual of her terrain. At that moment she recognized him perfectly. It was John the homeless. Totally different, with a different look. No disguise.

The third call in the theater was announced. Everyone was in their seats. The performance began and the actors took their part. But Laura and John were no longer mentally there. They were traveling in their telepathic space. Communicating between magnetic waves whose molecules conveyed an endless series of thoughts, in a short, nourished space, by a voracious audience in pursuit of a running scene.

Laura discreetly told her dad about who was sitting between the seats. He turned wisely, to ensure John's presence and to understand his daughter's unusual paroxysm. She didn't have a hard time imagining why John the homeless, was there. That indelible night her Chevy broke down, he asked for the book of Elena Garro that was in the back of her car, in compensation for repairing it when it broke down. A heavy day that ended on a crazy night. The night of a difficult day as the Beatles said quite a few decades ago. If there was one thing in common between them was precisely that. The literary interest of two writers, whose literature in the twentieth century had timed inside, unintentionally wanting to. Enjoying the play of the *poblana* was an event. No doubt. The ideal occasion for the unthinkable encounter.

La Garro sculpted her works, giving them a magical realism, close to the fairy tale. Splendid realism that overrides time and space, which leaps from logic to absurdity, from vigil to sleep. And that contemplates man and the world, with the ness of the mature and the candidness of the *parvulo*. The theatre where tragic irony reigns. Time, flight, and death are constants that occur in this environment. A spectacle that reveals a dream world, of subconscious illusions projected in the outlining of the human condition. Characters who are immersed in their crypt await the final judgment and ironically criticize life on earth.

The play was over, the applause that seemed unstoppable followed. Afterwards, all the attendees that had haste to leave, got lost heading for the corridors leading to the street. Laura's father, realizing the pressing situation, intentionally came forward with his wife and granddaughter, knowing that they would both be sought. Silently she thanked her father for complicity. John was not wasting time, he walked across the steps, evading out, people seeking the orderly escaped outwards. While Laura was waiting patiently. She looked laughing and surprised at the proximity of him. John was arriving to his goal by mocking the seats and without taking his eyes off, he asked:

"Laura, how are you?"

She couldn't answer that question that fast. Seeing him so closely. Groomed, clean, neat, very well dressed, presentable, worthy, animosity, strong, and even perfumed. He stunned her. His transformation shocked her. The beard was carefully trimmed. The face open and firm. His shiny shoes, tie, and sky-blue shirt. With a watch on his wrist. A distinguished man. So, she went straight to question it, not doing so would have caused her a hangover.

"Are you who I think it is? Or do you represent a ghost who likes theater and comes here to scare people away."

"You're not wrong. I'm the one you think is."

John, bold, took a couple more steps and thus could reach her aromatic breath. He sensed the delicious outflow of her perfume. So select and feminine. He thought her presence clouded other people's perception in the theater. She was a black beauty, with very clear divine eyes. Excited by her closeness, he sought her dark-colored arms by gently imprisoning them, he drew her to him. He scorned her slowly, solemnly, and prolongedly. She placed her face between his neck and shoulder. The lapels from his shirt received her cheek. He turned her into his possession. He surrounded her with all the length that his limbs allowed and squeezed her, like his pillow, sinking her fully into his chest cavity. They both hugged each other as if they were making love between the seats of the theater. Her parents without leaving the room and being on the threshold of one of the exits, witnessed what was happening with her daughter, who was falling apart before that man, like a chocolate at noon extended on the roof, melting for him. A tender and romantic scene. They saw them mingle, falling apart, melting, and consuming themselves in that unexpected encounter by sharing chunks of hope and desire.

Laura and Juan exchanged thoughts and ideas through the hug and warmth with which they communicated. Everything was inside them, their bodies said everything, without manifesting themselves in words. They sported their smiles to present each other their emotions and joy at the surprise of their prodigious find. Her white dress was lost in John's beige outfit, who looked like never before. Laura had long missed this moment that today was given away, with absolute vividness, surrounded the area with warmth, security, and enthusiasm. The hug lasted the same as the applause at the end of the play. It was a moment when the eyes closed, and the pulse accelerated the bliss of sharing one another. Milk and coffee. The water and the glass. Wine and the glass. Two in one to hold on, both in difficult times. A fraction without measurement. A drop of water stopped in space. A sigh faltering with the other. A breath turned into a prorogue. At last, she re-adapted and looked anxiously without warning her fellow pilgrim, inside her purse, a business card. She stretched it out and reproached him...

"I won't risk an upcoming appointment with no refund, here are my details. I'll be waiting for you. When you want to come to visit me, I will welcome you, whoever you are, I will be happy to hear you. Because I want you to know, I can listen, too."

He smiled at her with the magic of a judicious man, owner of an un yet spoken secret. He imprisoned her right hand with which she had shown the card, and he gave her a complimentary kiss as a farewell.

"Believe me, you beautiful brunette, I won't forget! I'll pick you up soon. You won't let me sleep!"

And without that being enough he murmured in her ear.

"Ah! No cameras, please. Because you'll scare the feline away."

When she heard him say that phrase "you won't let me sleep" she wanted to laugh. Beautiful feeling of being loved and thought out by him. I'm glad I'm not the only one suffering from insomnia, she said pleased. She gave John her coquettishness again and turned to see her parents who were still on the lookout, waiting for her. Laura walked to the end of the aisle to meet them and together they headed for the exit. Before getting lost among the people, in the right way, they sought for the last time in an act of reciprocity, pending their steps and sealing a new encounter in a tomorrow not dated on the calendar.

Driving the car on the road, her father looked at how happy she was. He was a co-pilot. Her beautiful Laura steered the wheel in a different manner. Her countenance picked up the features from her face, she smiled. Her mood moved. Enthusiasm boasted her happiness. He thought she would not have budgeted for this unusual encounter with the one who absorbed her ideas.

Suddenly Laura looked like another being. An obvious change had manifested itself in her, a candle lighting became a flashing lamp, with an unsuspended expression, her forehead opened and as a hurricane burst came new projects that opened doors that previously had closed. An innovative will took hold of her.

"Did you notice Dad, how much he changed?"

"Yes daughter, that man is a mystery. He looks very elegant in a suit and with a lot of personality."

"Yes, he is. He looks very manly and handsome, don't you think...?"

Her daddy smiled, looked away and lost in the memory of his deciduous youth, letting "his little girl" burst his imagination.

"Did you know father? He was in the Alameda that day he didn't show up."

"Did he tell you?"

"No, but he said it in a different way. He said in the end, no cameras please." It means that when he saw me with a camera hanging from my arm while I was waiting for him that afternoon, I frightened him, and he ran away. Now I know he was there, Father. I'm sure he almost yelled at me as I drove the car down the toll road, leaving the city of Monterrey. When he saw me with the camera, he didn't come up to me. It means this man is hiding from something, good or bad, I don't know. But I'm going to find out, you'll see. It won't be easy, but I'll find out."

"Watch out, Laura, that man can get you into big trouble. It gives me an I don't know what, to think that this gentleman doesn't want to show his true identity."

"Despite these ambiguities, Dad, I think he's a good man, after all, I smell it. My intuition tells me, he's running away from something, yes, but I don't think he's a criminal. Really, I doubt it very much. I hope I'm not wrong, because I'll be digging my own grave."

"How do you know he's going to pick you up?"

"Because now I was the one who threw a pager at him. A flirtatious woman who is interested usually catches her prey. We women have weapons that, without being belligerent, perform better than a rifle, or a punch fired by a male. He'll look for me, you'll see, when? I do not know. But he will."

CHAPTER V

Newton's third law says that with every action there is a reaction. Life is like a fronton game. You hit the ball and it comes back, or like the boomerang, you throw it up and it comes back. I think the human being himself is implicit in this law. Whatever you do in the course of your life, comes back, even if it may come back with another perspective, but in the end, it does. I remember well a book, later turned into a film, from many years ago that was called "*A Clockwork Orange*". The protagonists do and undo and violate what stands in front of them, but as the years go by, life takes its toll. Everything they did and provoked, will have them suffer in the same way. It is a novel by Anthony Burgess published in 1962 and released by British cinema in 1971. A barbarity of film. Although this was characterized by its violent, almost psychiatric content, it facilitates a social critique that fits perfectly in my particular life. Today you do one thing and tomorrow life takes your toll. That's right! That's why remembering what I was before and what I am now is a wheel of fortune. Sometimes you look at things from above, but other times, everyone looks down at you.

I'll start by saying I'm terrified of getting back involved with a woman. Last time I did, it was like a carnival. I even went to jail. First, I fell in love like a fool, of an impossible. I followed her for years, making myself worse off that she loved me the way I wanted her. I never got it. She married another slug, and I was left as a castaway in the middle of the ocean. Alone, with the sharks. I got a tremendous depression that I decided to end my life, to turn the light off for good. But the intent cost me a lot. All because I thought I'd go kill myself in a hotel that had a metal detector and I got caught in my room before I did my job. I was armed in the building, carrying the gun in the back of my pants. I documented myself at the front desk without problems. I looked for the elevator, went downstairs to room 325. I put the key in the lock, I opened it, I entered, I went to the bathroom to urinate, immediately after I looked for the bedside to prepare my outcome, and that's where I was, when suddenly three orangutans broke into the room, who presumed to be cops and unforeseen, they held me, beat me like I was a drug dealer or a criminal of those, very dangerous. They handcuffed me, pushed me out of the building on duty stairs, shoved me inside a cop car and I was in jail for eighteen months.

Indeed there, in that place, I was never going to be located by Rosario from who I was fleeing from, and I wanted to hide. Prison is the perfect place to go unnoticed by human rot. Nobody's looking for you. You're the garbage of the community. Your friends miss you, but no one would think of going to pick you up in jail. It's the last line of the notebook. Only a mother would pick you up, but not even my mother went, she died years ago.

Being inside, the cops who subdued me made it easy for them to accuse me of everything. They won't be able to! Okay! If that's what they live on, to raise false claims. They accuse the innocent to close a case. They charged me with attempted murder, for I don't know who. From carrying weapons owned by the army, to beating the law representatives (of course that was not true), and causing so much destruction in the hotel, which ones? I mean, doomed to spend three years behind bars. It's that easy. But as a server observed good behavior and excellent discipline, I was able to get out earlier than prescribed.

That misery to have lived that time locked up, really. You're having a hard time. You have plenty of time to reflect, think about what was and wasn't. The forced introspection exercises annihilate you by blaming you for everything your thoughts desire. Your surroundings are sad, grieffully, pitiful, rotten, and stinky. Your companions cry, count, recount, remember, curse. There's no horizon, it doesn't exist. There's no future in confinement. You only own the tortuous past from which you can't escape, because it has you cornered behind bars. Fuck! Worse than a nightmare. You scream without anyone listening to you, what you cry and implore doesn't matter to your neighbor. A neighbor who's probably more fucked up than you. Loneliness overwhelms you, doesn't let you sleep, you feel vulnerable, you're slaughtered, you're skinny. It takes little time to understand that you are alone among many who accompany you. You look at the calendar with as much anguish as if you were in the desert without water, and you'll be many miles away to reach the finish line. Hours don't pass, they park. The clock is your worst enemy. What's the point of you knowing that the sun has come up, if you don't see it. When it's raining, you don't have the privilege of getting wet. When it is night, when it is day, if it's Sunday or Christmas. It feels like shit. You're alone!

As in every society, prison also has particularities, there are oligarchies. Groups are formed to offend and attack; others to defend themselves and survive. Take care of your needs or belongings. As always, evil wants to subdue good. The biggest one sub judice the smallest one. Then he succeeds, even if he later loses it. Good defends itself from evil, but without being able to escape from it. On this matter I think the devilish angel won god's game. Evil is everywhere and good sometimes appears, but it comes to mend what has already damaged evil. The spaces are so small that it is impossible to run or take refuge away from the one that overwhelms you. Over time you understand that it will cost you your life to prevent yourself from being used by others. They abuse you, rob you, beat you, take you away, insult you and threaten you with death. Many times, they do, before any authority within the penalty helps you. It's not fatalism, it's reality. Prison is not only a symbol of bars and cloisters, but also a symbol of corruption, death, mistreatment, and dispossession.

Four months after being there, already consigned, and ready to serve a three-year sentence behind bars, I began to feel my customs within the context of which I was to live. Up at five in the morning. Clean up vomited floors, wash toilets full of shit, sweep and mop the dining room after all the inmates devoured their food. Help other colleagues in the boilers to keep them working, with a miserable heat worse than the one in Mexicali in the middle of August. I mean, very forced labor, so much so that, arriving at your bunk, you were charged in advance for all the effort of the day with a sleepless night.

The dormitories were classified. In one slept the drug dealer, and in another the murderers. Only we would have to distinguish one from each other, because some homicides were involuntary, and some were reckless. Sometimes one would come to think that some might have been necessary. Others in self-defense, that's why you couldn't and shouldn't cross them all out the same way. On the other hand, the ones who, if they received their true mistreatment, were the rapists. Because regularly those bastards abused their victims, and most of them were helpless beings. Therefore, when they were held in prison, we saw them as despicable and ruined beings. And the truth is, we misused our hands on them for being abusers.

It must be said that every prison stay has its price, and I would unknowingly pay mine, in a very cruel way. About ten months in detention, some scowl-faced men arrived at the prison. I don't know why the hell they were transferred, the thing is, they didn't go unnoticed. Immediately these bastards tried to intimidate everyone. There were four guys who then made deals with other colleagues, forming a real gang to subdue anyone in front of them. Strong, tall, hardened, and violent. Real bad guys, we were all afraid of them, in panic. Reason why it was no surprise to learn that sentries and prison guards were bribed and intimidated. At a later time, the inclination to forgive all their misdeeds was notorious. And my *Way of the Cross* began.

One of the many afternoons, after lunch, I was on my way to the outer courtyard of the criminal. To get out, you had to cross a kind of curved but elongated tunnel where the light of a low-powered spotlight illuminated the path weakly. Suddenly three of the bad guys became present and in my face, they told me with extreme cynicism that they were going to rape me. One of them was very clear when he threatened me. I'm going to stick my dick in, you son of a bitch, and you're going to feel really good. And you better get loose and be nice because if you don't, you're no longer going to be in existence here. That said, it was my time. I was already aware that the same thing had happened to other inmates. And you'd only save yourself if you loosened money ahead. It was the only way to clear the obstacle, but I didn't have any money.

I tried to run knowing it was useless. So, for the moment I pretended to be docile and made them believe that I had syphilis and AIDS. I invited them to consult with the prison health department. But my innocent lie didn't make any dents. They laughed with loud strident arguing that it was a very good strategy to save me from the situation, so now they were proposing another solution. Then you'll have to suck my pretty boy, said one of them. And the one next to him added. Me too. The screams, the stirs, the punches, the kicks, started and although I defended myself as I could, but at the end, they dominated me. I didn't give up, I didn't want too either. Even if I lost my life. I'd decided that much earlier, ever since I found out what happened to other inmates.

I was already bleeding from the face from the beating, held between two and they kept me crouched in the direction of the leader, he pulled out his filthy limb and threatened me by saying; kiss it idiot. At the time he had me with a dagger while he grabbed it with his other hand. I breathed as deep as I could again and again, and drawing strength from I don't know where, I kicked him in the nuts, his scream was heard all the way to the watchtower. Immediately the guy, with his genitals out fell to his knees, but also in that instant they accelerated the beating. I fell to the ground, and they kept kicking me until I no longer resisted. Thrown away and without conscious, I was no longer good for their purpose. The leader, who they called the *El Lobo* (The Wolf), was so angry that he was hurt, and that I fainted, he buried me in his dagger. His knife crossed my armpit and part of my chest, but I barely noticed because of my calamitous condition. My reality was beyond earth. I mean, they put me out of action. They left me there, tremendously beaten and stabbed, until later my cellmates helped me by taking me to the infirmary.

This unhappy attack kept me locked up in the infirmary for four weeks. Plastering the ankle of the right leg. With severe healings for the effects of stabbing in the chest. My body rigid on the stretcher holding my back in one position, because they had fractured two vertebrae. Plastered my nose by rupture of the septum. And since I had broken two ribs, I had a wide bandage around my chest, which surrounded the height of the navel. I mean, fucked up I couldn't be, I was alive by a miracle.

That's when there was a visit from important people to the prison. They were apparently officials doing an inspection of the facilities, as well as learning about the living conditions of the inmates. When they saw me lying there with everything that adorned me, they asked a lot of questions that I didn't miss an answer from. I must inform you that I had received a prior threat from an emissary of the Wolf, in case I opened my mouth saying details of the beating received. But I thought about the same thing as before. If from the previous experience I had come out alive, saying nothing now, was like signing my death sentence. So, I said it, and I said it all. With details. Place, space, time and who had been the executioners. Obviously, I also mentioned that the same thing had happened to other inmates.

Two months after that terrible trance, I fully returned to the prison cell. Now the bad guys were doing malice things without hiding, spitting out my food, or emptying something on it, pulling my hair when they passed near me, kicking me out of their inevitable closeness and leaving in my bunk bed poisonous animals or undesirable things like semen on the surface.

The Committee, who had visited weeks before, warned them personally, that if anything happened to me, they would go directly to their people and their condemnation would grow as much as the length of the country's northern border. I knew this information days after I joined the hostilities. That inspection also caused a significant change in three or four sentinels, causing the new members to be easily frightened and corrupted. At least they needed more time to achieve it.

Several weeks passed, I don't know how many, but they passed. One day, I don't know if I was lucky, I would think so, I witnessed a fact of which I'm still a prisoner of. The gang of bad guys that had formed in prison, and had shaken me, were connected to incognito drug dealers. My companions and I had imagined it since they arrived, but that day in total circumstantial form, I had stayed between two giant washing machines selecting clothes that remained pending. It was then that several of these guys appeared. They started yelling at each other, complaining about thousands of things that I didn't understand, threatening each other. Jail words. Suddenly, one of them who dragged an aluminum-colored trash can, put it up on a table where the inmates selected the laundry every day, whether white or colored, we used it. From the inside of the trash can, he extracted and showed the rest of the group large bundles of bills. Then, as if to assert what he was showing others, he emptied the can on the table and that's when I could clearly see many dollar bundles. As I glanced, I noticed a pile of riches. I was still crouching behind the washing machines. I was panicking that they would notice my presence, my legs were shaking. If they found me, they would kill me hopelessly. Suddenly, one of them pulled out a dagger and stabbed the guy who had emptied the money on the table three times. The irretrievable situation caused the other actors on the scene to lay on top, and among the six inmates they slashed themselves, which I don't know where they got the knives from, but they displayed them without any fear of being seen. Of all the inmates, four of them were left on the floor bleeding and complaining of wounds. The last two survivors finished stabbing the fallen. One of them, the Wolf, noticing that several wardens were approaching the squabbles, with the whistle in his mouth, ordered his companion to hide the loot, so he took the can, covered it with a quilt with which he at first sight stumbled and went to hide it under a well-folded clothes rack, where the one that was already clean was placed, and with other rags he saw on the ground in the first instance, out there lying around, he covered the pot with the money inside.

Oh! To my surprise, in front of the custodian, and when the one who had left the boat on the shelf reached the Wolf, he greeted him with a machete in the neck that almost ripped his head off the blow. That's where he lay next to the others. I mean, as they say, nobody knows who he works for. When the rest of the guards arrived, no one was at the scene, they all had fled. There were only dead people to pick up. The last guard signaled and urged the Wolf to leave. This one, somewhat hesitant, knew perfectly well where the money had been, so he thought, I would come back later for it. That's when I realized that, with security personnel in jail, the stay is more dangerous.

I was stunned, stupid, if I can say so. Stretching out my arms was a treasure. It was up to me to have it, easily. All I had to do was to have the courage and the decision to grab it, hide the money and be rich overnight. I was sure there was a respectable amount there. Besides, that wolf thug had tried to kill me and if it wasn't for the warning from the Inspection Committee on duty, he would have killed me by now, I was aware of it. But where do I hide it? And how do I keep it in storage until I get out of penalty? I leaned my back on one of the walls of the huge washing machine. I still didn't let myself be seen. Thinking about what to do with what I had just three steps away. What if I do this? What if I do the other thing? After all, it was revenge. The Wolf wanted to kill me, and if he knew what I saw today, he wouldn't hesitate to do it. I was urged to make a prompt decision, in that instant, because they would soon return the money. It was my chance. *"¡Tómame o Déjame!"*, Sang the Spanish group of *Mocedades* on a record that sold millions of copies. I had to think fast, but fast.

It was the first time I was in jail; I was forced to make a decision with an exaggerated speed. Supersonic. The concentration of my thoughts traveled at full throttle, calculating movements, actions, and situations that my mind would foresee in the immediate future. I put together experience, cunning, and balls at the same time, like they say, now or never. Because to rob the thief you had to have more than energy. Finally, and after thinking about it deeply in Einstein's style and its destructive formula, I decided to go down the dirt dump and its directionalities. First, cover the treasure in another kind of wrapper, then have another partner's complicity, trusting him, risking maybe he would steal from me, but well, there was no other way. And take the money out by keeping it in a safe place, but which one? Out of prison.

***

Several months later, and for good behavior, I saw myself on the street, walking like any passerby between the tumult, the cars, the noise, and the shops. I was in jail for a little over a year and a half. What a bitter, unpleasant, and depressing experience. People, when they wander the streets do not realize their freedom, until it's taken away from them. Well, they say no one knows what they have until it's lost. When they take away what you think is yours, that's when you realize what you had. How beautiful it is to walk without surveillance. See without being watched. Eat without your food being spitted at. Sleep alone with your body and thought, without anyone interrupting your solemn loneliness. You don't sleep in a bunk; you don't hear the neighbor barking or snoring neighbor who doesn't shut up all night. Freedom is the most precious treasure of humans and we do not realize it until we lose it. That's ironic. To be slaves to our own libertarian thinking. Freedom is not only in the soul, it's also in what accompanies us. The freedom to think and decide, to love and to select, to choose and to take.

You don't buy that. *Fernando Savater* said, choosing is freedom to be and to have, because all our lives we are choosing, selecting, and electing for our lives. Who lives better is because he's chosen better.

Getting out of jail and going home was impossible. They'd wait for me there for sure. I couldn't drive my car; I couldn't find my address. They'd keep an eye on everything I did. They sensed that I knew where that money was and that's why I felt watched all the time. The Wolf inquired, researched, asked, and launched himself thoroughly to conclude that at least I knew who had taken all those wads of bills. They wouldn't leave me alone. They were going to chase me tomorrow, afternoon, and night and wherever I was. And when they managed to get the loot in their hands, they'd kill me.

Hopelessly and without over sinking, I launched into the streets as a homeless person to confuse and depress the idea that I was the intellectual author of stealing their money. I let my beard grow, I made some electrician boots that without capping at the tips I could walk in all comfort. My hair grew, I tied it with some shoelaces in the first instance and then with cords that I had found in the streets. I bought my backpack when I got out of prison and my clothes were from a worker's who I managed to buy from an outside factory in Apodaca. At first, it was pitiful and painful sleeping on the street. With the cold and tolerating the mosquito bites that do not leave you calm, but tiredness overcomes you and you learn to master the discomfort of insects in your body. Walking in the street, nobody listens to you. Homeless people are like ghosts that have a body and volume, but they are invisible to people. Nobody listens to you, no one sees you and if they do ignore you as if you were part of a landscape lost among many. People's eyes are used to seeing only what they are looking for and not what is in their environment. If I didn't adopt this life, I'd be without it. They would have taken my money anyway.

I go to the DIF Family Integral Development offices from time to time to help me. I told them that my name is John. A John who no one interrogates. An unknown John, or disguised, or of the whores, or John from the street. I mean like an unimportant John. I bathed without shaving. Sometimes I wash my underwear. I sit at the table to eat until I get fed up and go out again two days later, to look outside for what I don't have inside. When I can I get a book or two. It's a pleasure to read. Reading is living by learning. It's my escape, it's my safe conduct, it's the knowledge that comes through my brain and reaches the well of my existence. Reading is saving what you've learned as if it were a library where you store words on shelves. I was imprisoned in a prison in the north of the country, which is why I went to a nearby town like Saltillo so I wouldn't be too far from what's mine, when I say about what's mine, I'm talking about what I love. My house, my stuff, my books, my car.

The stacks of bills came out two days after the sanction. The garbage truck was responsible. The wrapper was bulgy and boring. It had no mark or color. That was the sign. A muddy, resistant plastic that could be preserved for a while outdoors. I was good friends with the garbage truck driver. Having chosen him was no coincidence, there was a friendly fund in the vicinity. He had once been imprisoned and knew the world of prison lockdown. We understood each other as well as the book and the reader. Knowing what everyone thought, our talks were very illustrative. And precisely by coming to him, I asked him in secret, to keep the wads of dollar bills, which I hid in a special can and that I notified him through a sign. They were in the can coming out of the dorm section.

After the robbery I thought my friend, the dumpster driver, was going to disappear from the world map, but no, I was wrong again and when I was released, I looked for him, he had me guarded in custody. He'd already grabbed something. I gave him the rest of his share and I kept mine. Until then, I knew how much we'd both been touched. For him it was three hundred thousand dollars and for me, seven hundred thousand more. (I don't understand yet, how such a large amount of money was hidden in prison.) In America this amount is minuscule, but in mine it was enough money to have a good time for several years. He was left with something else for sure, but, well, rewarding the individual's faithfulness in some way was to show him my appreciation for his contribution in the crucial moment of events. I said goodbye to him with a big hug and wished him the best of luck from there on out. Days later, he quit his job as a garbage truck driver. Nobody said anything, I never saw him again.

I went to wander the streets of Saltillo. A city that has a sensational climate compared to any other in northern Mexico. For example, between two cities like Monterrey and Saltillo that are an hour away, in times of summer, there is a big difference in the thermometer, about five degrees Celsius. While a shadow in Saltillo is a blessing, in Monterrey you perceive it as if you were under the sun's rays. And not to say the city of Nuevo Laredo, that's where you roast.

Saltillo seems to me more provincial, less tumultuous, and organized and orderly, to live with a little more calm and patience, without reaching the discomfort of the city stress. Instead, Monterrey is a whole metropolis, impetuous, constantly noisy, conflicted, full of action. That's why I chose Saltillo to settle in its entrails. So, I spent a little over two years hiding among the columns of the uneven steps. Protecting myself under the shade of tall buildings, going to sleep at times to the premises of any Social Welfare unit and approaching people who could somehow help me.

And right now, after all these years, Laura appeared. A night when her little car broke down and it didn't want to start anymore. The night she looked crazy in the dark. She lost her sanity, and I admired her madness. There are things that are difficult for women, I don't say impossible, but in male hands they are easy to solve. For the most, no misogyny. But the truth is, there will always be things that only man can handle.

How do I tell her that I like her? That she is a woman who meets my expectations? How do I let her know my feelings without getting naked when I propose it? If even, I don't know if the time to be hiding is prudent, or the thug "Wolf" has already resigned himself to losing his money. From a good source, I know that bastards very well connected. A guy used to stealing doesn't let him lose a million dollars that easily. In that operation there was embezzlement, deceit, death, murder, and commitment. I know, that's why coming to hide among the streets of the capital of the Mexican state of Coahuila was my salvation, reason to keep me alive.

Was I doing the right thing letting myself be seen by a woman who I liked? I'm now forty-four years old. Was I right to be attracted to a Beatrice who questioned me? I'm not blind, and it's not my first time. She likes me and I'm to her liking. But will it be all right, let me swing over these student-looking flirtations? I haven't gotten out of one prison and I'm already getting into the other. I'm just freeing myself from the clutches of a failed love with Rosario, also wanting to forget about a killer who would give everything to find me. Would it be all right, to let me hunt for a woman who I find interesting? What to do? Open myself up? And let everything happen naturally? How good will it be to entrust my life to a woman I don't know?

CHAPTER VI

It's not easy to live in today's globalized world. Competition has led us to the abyss of dehumanization. Man unfolds in a disorderly and unjust environment, where violence is a finding witnessed by any conscience. He's a slave to his own freedom. A slave-enslaved, violently enslaved freedom. In universities, teachers are committed to teaching their students that freedom is discovering themselves. They show how to recognize the field of action of their limits and capabilities. Because freedom is to be able to establish a social relationship with any fellow man, understood as this one, as freedom to act and move to any cardinal point. I mean, power and wanting to go where you want, that's the freedom sought. Is there such freedom today? At least in my city, it doesn't exist.

Today, on any street or road you are assaulted, kidnapped, and robbed, as if stripping the other away was eternal salvation. Just as vampires do to prolong their lives, one wants to take away from the other what he has earned, what belongs to him. Today's Mexican humanity has lost its values. It's ill-intentioned, proud, and fraudulent. There's no security anywhere anymore. Not even at home. Freedom has been amputated by that space to function, where it sits in its field to give security. At the beginning of the 21st century there was a freedom imprisonment by undivided men who, in their fantasy for survival, crack, strip goods and remove the root of good. Perversity has broken the border lines of human quality, to become irrational beasts wandering in the middle of the street. In daylight. Not just in my city, but all over the world. He has returned to the times of barbarism.

Charles Baudelaire in *Flores del mal* says that evil is done effortlessly. Naturally. For fatality, good is always the product of an art, everything that is beautiful and noble, is the result of reason and calculation. And he adds to my astonishment: *that the background of the human being is always dark and evil.* That only art is capable of painting and building a habitable world.

I'm definitely with him. I cannot guarantee whether we once inhabit a more barbaric world; I mean the *World Wars* of the twentieth century, or today, with the constant and endless riots in the streets of any metropolis. Let it be known, all over the world. Is it true what the Frenchman *Pierre Boulle* predicted one day. That the world would end up being inhabited by apes? If I have a story to tell about my city, I'll say the world is still alive. As alive the homeless man who in his metamorphosis surprises anyone.

December was dying on the annual agenda. He lived his last hours. Christmas had its fruits and just on the *day of the innocent,* in the afternoon, the opportunity presented itself for the homeless man to become accountable to the licensed professional. Still in office hours he went up to the corresponding floor, as marked by the business card he carried in hand. Arriving, he went to the reception to announce himself. The secretary receptionist announced it by telephone extension and said what the visitor had warned her.

"Yes, ma'am, he says he's who he appears to be, but is not. He tells me his name is *John the homeless*. You tell me if I let him pass."

Laura's countenance, then, showed a smile that bounced all over the walls.

Just three weeks had passed since the theater meeting in the city of Monterrey, and he was coming to look for her. She even turned the glass that divided the building with the abyss towards the surrounding street. Laura needed to think of what to do. She was an hour away from meeting her work schedule. And she did something unusual, she spoke to her immediate boss on the phone and warned her that because of a very important personal matter, she was going to be absent for the rest of the afternoon. She hung up, took her purse, and left her office.

The restaurant where they went was elegant and sober. My city offers that kind of advantage. There's everything, like in the pharmacy. The place has a hint of French, they offer category wines, good school stews and the clientele that frequently go is highly selective. Not everyone can cover the tab after dinner.

"I'm glad you accepted my invitation, Laura. The truth is, I owe you a lot of explanations."

"Don't worry, I owe you some too. However, you should've told me you were coming. No! On second thought, it was better that way. I would have been impatient all day. Fearing you'll stand me up again. How horrible it is to wait in vain. It's awful. I had a hard time that afternoon at the Alameda, you know?"

"Excuse me, but in the course of our talk you will know why I did not attend that Saturday. Besides, let you know? No! That's what it was all about, to catch you by surprise. I have so many things to tell you. I hope you're like an open book."

Better than that, I'm a tape recorder. I've got as much time as you want. I've let my parents know I'd go out with you. And even though they were worried, I feel it was better to do so. I just hope you don't think about kidnapping me today.

They both laughed with the nonsense. I'm sure they would have a nice time. They looked carefree, content, relaxed. And with a mountain of questions to be asked. They ordered a couple of glasses of red wine, ordered their plates, and with a talking incontinence, they were departing like two arrows by the event. Even though John, the homeless man was known that this time he was going to lose his identity. So, without preamble Laura went straight to the point.

"For the time being, I want you to answer the first question, which has had me entangled this entire time. In all truthfulness. Who are you? And from whom are you hiding? And please, this time I don't want evasiveness, no amazing love stories, I beg you."

He started by telling her his real name: "My name is Edgar". He told her his date of birth and all his general details. He went on with the rest. Born in San Luis Potosí, his age, his studies, his work record, experience in other needs. He had to repeat his failed love for Rosario and immediately afterwards began to tell her the thorn of the story. imprisoned for a while, the ravages of being beaten and finally getting out of prison with money hidden in a trash can. He had escaped the clutches of a very bloodthirsty and cursed thief, enough, to have him killed if he found out he had stolen his money. He also told her that to lose sight of him and save his life, he found himself in need of hiding for more than two years in the street, under the ignominious personality of a homeless man. A divergent life, protected with the veil of a severed, stray and vague being, but that in the end that disguise gave him peace and security. And on the other hand, it left him a huge apprenticeship of life and its passages, in the lowest strata of society. He narrated to her in detail the different situations he endured in those quite difficult living conditions. Hunger, dirtiness, rottenness, coldness, loneliness, silence and annoyance etcetera. He told her how he sheltered himself with cartons, sometimes lying next to other filthy people who approached him to accompany him during the night. He was afraid of being photographed by the authorities of any unit. To some journalist or reporter. Afraid his face would be published in newspapers or on television. Which is why he was always running away from those events where the police would show up, whether it's in a street robbery, or in a house, a car crash, or anything like that.

He also told her that he would go alone to any Charitable Association. He did it for a bath and a little clean up. He was going fast just like he walked in, just like he was going on. In addition, he had his appearance show the ravages of the revealed, the inclement weather on the skin and that his hair grew enough to cover his face. In fact, every time he appeared before any health institution, he released his hair to make his appearance even more deplorable. He wanted to disguise himself as a perfect stranger.

"Captivating what you're saying. Interesting, but dangerous. I finally know your name."

And she went back to harass him with more questions.

"And you think, Edgar, I'm going to believe you this easily? Am I going to swallow this story completely again? How do I know you're telling me the truth?"

"Because this time I speak to you with my heart in my hand, really. I'm not in disguise this time. I'm not lying to you. I'm not hiding anything. This time I show myself authentic, before you, completely naked. At that point, he removed his driver's license and I.D. from his wallet to corroborate it. I have no parents, no children, and no wife. And I've decided to share all this with you, because I know, through your eyes, that we could be friends to trust each other for the future that awaits us."

"So now you're a psychiatrist?! How do you know that I want to be your friend?"

"Because I know you, you wouldn't have agreed to go out with me. It's that easy!"

Again, both countenances were eclipsed, finding themselves in the path of magnetized glances. His right hand stole Laura's left and carried it to his mouth, to kiss her palms. And he added afterwards, she was the only window left to open.

"Please don't let me go! I beg you! Let me get closer to your life. Be pious with my truth, it's not cynicism! I have a feeling you're a one-piece woman, but right now what I'm trying to do is reach your heart."

And with that being said, he asked:

"Would you be able to have a romantic relationship with me? Would you accept this poor tramp as your driver from now on? Because I want to bring you, take you. Be in all the places you move to and be your protector. What do you say?"

After the romantic request a simultaneous silence was opened, almost agreed. They didn't say anything. They raised their glasses, toasted. His hands were shaken without express request. Everyone governed their movements, but in the atmosphere of that table there was a responsible, united, and supportive agreement without even uttering a conjugated verb on a compromise.

Edgar was warm and took off his coat. He was wearing a different suit than last time. His tie had vivid greens with gray stripes that encircled from the neck to the buckle of his belt. White shirt, cufflinks. She could not see his eyes directly, without first colliding with golden-framed lenses. His hair undulated over his forehead with a tiny fringe that bathed him in youth flanked by a smile.

"Now you tell me, just as I have. What about your life? Tell me, I'll hear you. And why do you always wear white, it makes you look more beautiful every time I see you."

She also, without hiding anything from him, began to tell him, her past and present. Habits, customs, her work in the office, failed marriage, divorce. Her daughter Marianita. The beatings she suffered from her husband's fists. The gorilla she was married to. She still wanted to tell him that she was also a professional and liked her job very much. She was already a few years old as an editorial manager, that is, she was lucky for her seniority. She also told him about the transcendence of her parents. Her Mexican dad and her mother of Moroccan descent. They met on the U.S. border with Mexico, on the side of Laredo, Texas. Lost among so many people who come in and out of both countries. At that time my mother was hiding from the border patrol, she said, my mother had no relatives to go to. No money to survive. Her companion with whom she was traveling with had died of starvation. My father, seeing her alone, offered her a home and sustainment, and she agreed. Over time and a hook, things got better. They came to Saltillo, bought a house and had me, taking care of me until now. And... regarding the white color. It's my favorite color. In fact, it has always been. White is the headboard of my bed, the quilt, and my sheets. As you can see, so is my car. My closet only has white clothes and I try to buy similar clothes, to look like I always wear them. It's a trap for the eye of the one who admires me. Because I know my dress arouses comments. I do it with all intent.

So, I'll be friends with a white image!

Having put all the words about the context of a nascent romantic relationship, the two were seen with another optician. Their perspective changed both on one side to the other. After a while, the questions ran out and they chatted unhindered. Laura suddenly crossed her legs and leaned her elbows on the table in a clear sign of pleasant complacency on hearing him. He moved from the chair from time to time to strip his bottom of some discomfort. None of them lit up a cigarette, it seemed that smoking was not to their liking. And so, they spent the evening, in an exchange of ideas and plans without conditioning their tastes. The bill was paid for by him, in cash. True to his custom, Laura surprised him.

"Will you be busy on New Year's Eve? Where are you going to spend it? We could give you asylum at home. Maybe God will reward us for feeding a homeless man."

"You ask a lot of questions that only have one answer. I told you. I have no family, no place to go. Of course, I'd like to be with you that night with your family. Actually, I was going to ask you. Those solemn and ceremonial days, I spent them twice behind bars, others on the street or in anonymity."

They said goodbye with a hug surrounded by promises, a kiss on the cheek, with a described address and an invitation for December 31.

***

It was the last day of December, 9 o'clock at night. Dinner was ready, the table was set up, two bottles of wine were distinguished between the dishes of a white tablecloth, well ironed and without missing a bottle of cider for the New Year toast. Smiling parents. Laura was anxious, restless. Her little girl was running back and forth, not knowing she would have a visitor, so when the doorbell rang Marianita screamed loudly, "I'll get it! I'm coming!" And she opened the door smiling. With open arms and a splendid smile, she looked at a man with a well-groomed black beard and tie and with a bouquet of flowers on his hands.

"I'm looking for your mom. Is she home?"

Without saying anything else, little Mariana left the door wide open so that Edgar was able to see how fast she ran to the end of the house, to give notice of who knocked on the door. The girl went to her mother's lap to tell her that someone was looking for her, screaming to the sky, without stopping her insanity.

"Mom, Mom!" A person is looking for you at the door! He's a gentleman with a beard."

Edgar stood at the threshold of entry, waiting for an older person to make his appearance. Laura assumed who was at the door. She was already expecting it. Of course she expected it! If he had missed tonight, she would've never forgiven him. It was a special night for everyone. The father kindly went to the door to meet the one who asked about his daughter. He found a well-dressed man, in a black, elegant, bow suit at the neck, polished shoes and an open bouquet of roses overflowing with his forearm.

"Sir, good evening, I'm looking for Laura, is she home? Edgar said, very respectfully."

The father, aware of the sentimental adventures of his daughter and aware of the visit that came, was condescending with whoever tried to enter the house and invited him to cross the threshold, opening the door wide. The father led him to the living room. There, Laura came upon him. A discreet hug and a kiss on the cheek of rigor was the welcome that opened the space where both would share that family night. She was grateful for the colorful bouquet of roses that accompanied him and then went to the kitchen to get a vase and place that colossal bouquet of red buttons. After the first dabbling, they dined, laughed, conversed between a barrage of questions and answers that shot up in every direction. Of course, Edgar was the target of Laura's parents. They asked him a little about everything, and he calmly answered every doubt they had. Obviously, the prison chapter had been closed. That was top-secret. They had agreed not to share it with the parents.

New Year! New Year! Everyone yelled. Hugs here and there. Grapes, cheers, toasts, wishes, promises and tears appeared on the faces of the commensals except for Mariana's, who saw how her mother was distracted by the man who now kept her entertained. Laura didn't care much about it. And the effect surprised her. But Edgar realized the situation. So, he asked for permission to go to his car, reasoning that he had forgotten something inside. When he returned, he was holding a beautifully plastered Walt Disney storybook in his hands with a striking-colored cover.

The book was heavy enough to hold it with both hands. A collector's item. It was distinguished by a red ribbon that served as a page divider. He gave it to the little princess of the meeting, telling him that Santa Claus had mistakenly gone to his house and had left the gift in his hands, with the holy commission to deliver it to the girl Mariana.

"By any chance, Are you that girl?"

"Yes, it's me! My name is Mariana! Right mom?"

Her daughter was so excited that without preamble she kissed Edgar and offered him her happy and joyful childish face. The gift really impacted the little girl. She immediately went upstairs to her room, carrying her book with effort. With the treasure in her hands, she disappeared from the scene. Mariana, being alone, saw it, skimmed through it, and admired the main figures and drawings. After a while, she came back still excited about the colors, the title, drawings, and the Disney tales. She went towards Edgar's legs, sitting on the edge of the main sofa in the living room, the little girl said to him in front of everyone, with her little warm voice, but sonorous:

"I want you to be my new dad!" You are a very good person.

And she threw herself with open arms towards Edgar who received her stunned, shy, and speechless for the girl's sudden frankness. No doubt she had been pleasantly surprised by that children's storybook. Everyone was stunned by Mariana's unusual expression. Surprised. What she had said left them thunderstruck, speechless. Mainly to Laura who thought, what did she mean by *"I want you to be my new dad*?" But where had that nonsense come from? How could a being as young as five years old say that? And without fully understanding her baby, she wondered then, her real dad, whom she saw every month? Where had he been? That's awful! What a crazy thought!

That apparent insanity of the little girl had a reason. Every time she asked her, it was her father's turn to see her, as the conditions for the divorce claim stipulated, he questioned her: Who is your mother with? What has she done? Where did she go? Who has she been with? Her father would even shake her and intimidate her, if she did not inform him of everything her mother did, inside and outside the house. The girl as she could, answered her executioner's requests. Yeah, between father and daughter they shared time together, but during that span, the idea of being friends was distant. He would put her in a store to eat any craving or distract her among the arcade games at some mall. He was busy with his cell phone all the time and to prevent his daughter from distracting him, he would buy her unimportant things. So, Oscar entertained her more by obligation than by the feeling of fraternity.

For that reason, Mariana was so loquacious and sincere to declare her an admirer like Edgar. To the point of inviting him to be her daughter's new dad. No one had given her anything to impress her so much. Something that surpassed her imagination. And Edgar had guessed right and knew exactly what she liked.

"Are you a magician? How did you know I liked *Snow White and the seven dwarves?*" Mariana asked him immediately afterwards.

"Well, easy. Seeing your mom who's a smart, talented person. I said, she must be, like mother like daughter" And looked at her face trying to see if the girl would figure out what he wanted to tell her. "I mean, if your mom is beautiful and charming, then I thought; the daughter must be the same, don't you think?"

"Well, yes! Of course!" The girl replied immediately, at the time when everyone laughed at the prompt response of the girl who evoked the comedian *chavo del ocho.*

But the joys didn't stop there, because soon after the girl added:

"Do you want to read me a story?"

"Of course I do. I'd really like to. What story do you want me to read?" Edgar quickly replied.

Ever since he bought the book, he's been planning that moment. Befriend the only person who could be his enemy to get to Laura's heart. The benevolent plan had paid off. So now, he looked very pleasant, reading the story of *Snow White and the seven dwarves* to the protagonist of that New Year's Eve night.

The evening went by on that. The girl asked at two o'clock in the morning, as if Edgar were Santa's envoy, for him to come up to her bedroom, to read to her other tales containing the blissful gift. The others volunteered for such a pediment, but the little girl in love at the time insisted with all her energy that the reader would be the guest. Edgar did it very willingly. He read several. One after the other, until the girl fell asleep with her little hands in his arms. Without proposing, it had been a childishly marvelous night. On the opposite side of the girl's bed, Laura always waited, for her homeless man, converted into St. Nicholas, to finish reciting the entrusted work.

Living the moment so close to the child reading incident provoked a great emotion in Laura's feelings. She adored Edgar's tolerance and patience so as not to complain about his time and give the right dimension to her daughter's candid needs. That left her engrossed. She called him possessing an extremely pleasant, tolerant, and paternal temperament. To allow with extreme parsimony the restlessness of reading to her daughter with everything and her daily whims, was to go beyond what was thought by this man who, each time, was shown with greater qualities to be loved by her. She thought with some envy, that now there were two who were in love with the same man.

The clock hit half past 3 in the morning. Edgar thought it was time to say goodbye. He appreciated the invitation, left home with the good wishes of the family, and set out to board his car. Laura, without detaching herself from him, followed him until he opened the door. Edgar had every intention of kissing her passionately, but her parents wouldn't take their eyes off him, so he left it for the next occasion.

"I've had a truly amazing evening. You have a beautiful, envied family. I'd like to belong to it!"

Oh my God! "I'd like to belong to it!" Laura heard him say that perfectly well. This man has been making me fall in love through my ears. There's no doubt about it. His words and actions are like a being from another galaxy. Accurate, punctual, and worthy of someone special and unpredictable.

They hugged, kissed, flirted with each other like good friends and said goodbye without wanting to. The night had been sensational and unforgettable. A feeling had been born that would hardly be erased. She with her everlasting white and he with his black suit wished a good night. Laura saw him drive away in his Ford and head for Carranza Avenue. She still didn't know where he lived, but now she didn't care about that detail, she knew he was coming the next weekend.

CHAPTER VII

Laura's parents met in 1975 completely accidentally. At the time her father worked for a Customs Agency whose work purposes were the transfer of goods to both sides of the border. He held the position of Operating Manager of the company, constantly crossing between the border floors of the United States and Mexico.

The border became familiar ground for Juan José documenting transfers, supervising the traffic of goods, executing, and carrying out customs procedures, working meetings in the groups and confirming that the warehouse had no lags in its stock. Being Nuevo Laredo one of the most frequently used borders in the constant management of imports and exports, it was essential to have professional people and aware of the activities to be completed daily. However, shipments continuously showed deviations, errors, or losses. And JJ (as his co-workers called him) gave agility to processes and transfers. Customers, being normally demanding, wanted everything to go smoothly from the first shipment instances. It wasn't always like that, though. Day-to-day life was a daily injection of headaches. But there's no way he would give that up, he reflected. Anyway, he was used to dealing with that problem.

One day after the thirty days the month of June has, with a shaded temperature of 45 degrees Celsius (113 Fahrenheit) and in line with his pickup to cross the bridge, JJ saw Layla, as he later knew her name. She was sitting on the side of one of the fences. She was a black woman, beautiful, with almost greenish gray eyes, with her hair mingled like a large cotton skein on her head. JJ was driving the company's vehicle bound to Laredo Texas when he looked at her not so far from his reach.

It wasn't common to see a black woman alone, with an old suitcase and a box next to her legs, sitting, wrapped with a sad image in the eyes of any driver. Crossing the Rio Bravo for many pedestrians would daily happen, but seeing a woman alone sprawled in one of his fences, in all truthfulness, it caught the eye. He found it strange to see her in that position, but, well, at least he thought it was ordinary to see young people at the border crossing that being surprised by the U.S Border Patrol, they were returned to their country.

He crossed the bridge. While on the other side, he did his job at the relevant office, considering urgent matters of a jammed boarding on the American side. When he got back, three hours later, he resaw over the same fence of the bridge, the same woman sitting right in the place where he had looked before, but this time, paying more attention, a few tears would slide on her cheeks like a toy-less girl. His truck was driving past the right lane, so he had it so close that he could see her features three yards away from the steering wheel.

He ended up crossing the adjoining bridge. He parked his car on the first sidewalk he saw free, and walked back to the place where the woman was. She, with a rag-like handkerchief, rubbed her wet cheeks. JJ did not hold back, he went straight to the point, and offered to help her. He did not get an immediate response, but he respectfully insisted until the lady agreed. She told him that she was alone, that her companion had disappeared, and for that reason she had no money to spend the next few days. She was desperate. She didn't know what to do.

Juan Jose thought when his eyes adjoined her closeness; "this woman is truly beautiful." JJ invited her to lunch so he wouldn't look ambitious or vulgar. He first spoke to her in English, and she answered more or less easily to his questions. Then he did it in Spanish and although he also understood it well, he caught her in severe holes with her pronunciation. But hey, JJ got his talk along the way of good things to come. Their topics were handled between the two languages, and they entered a conversation that opened the door to a world unknown to both.

It had been more than 36 hours and she had not tasted food. She really enjoyed what the waitress put on her table. Juan José took her to a small restaurant on Guerrero Street, a popular place where they cooked with homemade tortillas. There they ate sopes, tacos, and quesadillas, as well as other very Mexican cravings, which she loved.

That's how a long story was born to tell. She's 35 and he's 39. The adventure went to the time and space of Nuevo Laredo. A city created from castaways who worked only to achieve a transient antiquity in a factory and as soon as it acquired a home and a trade, it was quickly headed towards the United States.

That night and the next seven he took her to stay in a furnished house located a few blocks from the downtown area. The flirtation that JJ initiated was from the beginning allowed by her. In fact, she never saw with bad eyes the aspect of her unexpected companion, who from the first attempts devoted himself to caring for her and taking care of her as if she were the only woman on the border.

She, initially shy, and JJ extremely respectful of his new friend, began a relationship that, from the previous circumlocutions, was to be prolonged. For a long season they lived together on the Mexican side of the border. They settled in the neighborhood of *Colinas del Sur*. Over the months, other plans emerged, and their course changed dramatically.

Her name was Layla. Two or three times she narrated to him, until he learned that she had studied the equivalent of high school. She then found a man she married, and newly married, had traveled with her spouse from Morocco to the United States in search of peace and a better quality of life. They had no children after four years of marriage. It was a couple leaping around the world, indeed, but attracted by the American country with the greatest socioeconomic virtues from all continents.

They had crossed through Cuba and from there by raft, they arrived to Miami. They went into American soil with twenty thousand dreams on their forehead. Their initial adventure led them to Boston and where they parked. Her husband devoted himself to working on anything and whatever, teaming up with a group of also undocumented Latinos. As a waiter, or a cook in any restaurant, or as a glass cleaner, gardener, chauffeur. Her husband had to learn Spanish to communicate with his fellow human beings to integrate into the working conditions. And what better way of speaking it on the daily, to sign it, with repetitions of the memory and with jostles, but he managed to stay with them. That's how they started to get acquainted with the Spanish language. In turn, arriving at his abode, he broadcasted the news to his wife in the same language.

Layla saw little of her partner because every day he would be late and tired. Sometimes he worked on missions, which even took place outside the area where they kept their home. That's how they remained for two years. But it just so happened that one day living in New York, her spouse no longer came home. She waited for him quietly, with tremendous fear and without leaving the house for two weeks until her pantry was extinguished, and so hunger forced her out. She went as far as her husband was supposed to work, but nothing. She also asked her acquaintances, and nothing. With misfortune and with grief no one knew of her spouse's fate. She went to find her undocumented friends her husband's friends, but they also were unaware of his whereabouts, though, they helped him find work in a restaurant. However, luck was not on their side, weeks later their employer told them that the Border Patrol agent was about to inspect the premises. He asked them to leave quickly. Anyway: The Border Patrol grabbed them all. Layla ran out of money, no papers, helplessness, no man by her side, no friends. She preferred to lie by arguing to have relatives in Mexico thinking that her peers would help her reach her destination. But when the time came, her friends had deaf ears and left her to her fate.

This is how she arrived to the Nuevo Laredo Bridge that day, when JJ saw her grieving over one of the rails of the international bridge of the Bravo River. Thus, Layla spent two and a half years wandering around the United States until the time Laura's father helped her.

It would have been useless for someone from her home country to have tried to help her. Morocco is on the other side of the world; JJ humbly told her when they had already struck friendship. So, Juan Jose's sudden appearance at the border had been a real blessing. He provided her with protection, security, and shelter so that she would feel spoiled and calm. What pleased her the most was that her man always respected her. He gave respect from the beginning and treated her throughout her relationship as if she were his wife.

Already living together, JJ saw that Layla was pregnant, so he decided to give up his job at the border and move to Saltillo. A city that received them with a much more benevolent climate. An orderly, clean northern capital without so many tumults. Quiet and with her full belly to the brim, she stepped on the emblem of *Sarape de Saltillo* at the expense of her husband who had since protected her and cared for her as if she had found the other half of her orange. They had their baby girl who was born kicking and screaming openly in one of the hospitals in the city center. "Negrita" (a sweet nickname) he said, you gave me a girl, bless you, I owe you, my life. A Moroccan and a Mexican gave birth to a girl in the State of Coahuila, who was baptized as Laura.

Juan José, already with a family on his back and being in the capital, specified his way of life and sought his maintenance responsibly. For his fortune and at that time, the signing of the Free Trade Agreement, between the USA and Mexico, favored Coahuila's socio-economic conditions. A situation that the State took advantage of in its energy resources, industrial culture, technological education, and border statehood, to boost the economy, therefore reached significant growth in the 1990s. The promotion of the State to take advantage of the new conditions of the Treaty captured a significant investment of several million dollars and the installation of about 200 companies mainly of foreign origin. So, JJ did not suffer to be employed in a large company, and thus strengthened his economic aspirations to be a strong pole in the protection of his family.

They bought a house. Over the years they acquired good furniture, and from time to time they traveled to the interior of the Mexican Republic to be in contact with the historical roots of the country. Layla never returned to her native country, Morocco.

In fact, she had thanked God, in her new religion, for having found a solid, promising, and happy future, alongside a man who loved her from the first day he helped her on the border of the Two Laredo's.

Layla knew that in her homeland she would have suffered all kinds of abuse and humiliations. She was telling her JJ. It's awful to live in starvation. Because today, according to experiences, humanity resembles a piece of concrete that has no root. She assured that the development of violence that causes hunger, wars, and social disintegration, is a violence with weapons of mass destruction and whose victims are volatilized. I wonder, she said to herself, where are the university minds with the Utopian window of freedom? "If freedom is prison today." And she kept: in universities there is a drive towards intellectual, ethical, and aesthetic development. The goal of these is to go towards the knowledge of the cosmos and the human soul. Preserve the intellectual, artistic and spiritual legacies of the past, and open new possibilities to knowledge and imagination." Unfortunately, these chimeras are only the pretensions of someone who wants to live in peace, and desire times that they may never be able to witness this. For this reason, what was now living in Mexico, a more or less healthy country, referring to its economy, and without the ravages of a life at war, besides having her husband retired, seeing her beloved daughter happy, and hugging her granddaughter; was a gift that life had given her, in payment to her unease.

CHAPTER VIII

Oscar woke up after five o'clock in the afternoon on the first day of the month. The restlessness, the hangover and hunger made him open his eyes. He was surprised when he saw a girl lying next to him. He barely remembered who she was. The girl didn't even notice when he yawned loudly sitting on the side of the bed. He turned to all the walls of the room to notice where he was at the time. Gradually, lucidity came to his brain and filled its contents with the memory of his outrageous friends. The drink at the tables, the whiskey flying from hand to hand, the girls toasting with them, the meat grilling, the music at full volume and the smoke of the cigars forming clouds between jubilant faces. After toasting the New Year, they played "spin the bottle" among the participants. Spinning it and depending on the direction in which the tip of the bottle landed, the person in front asks the person in the back questions, which had been agreed in the game. A garment, a kiss, a hug, a poem, a song or even eating a cigar. They had agreed to bet on clothes. So, little by little and one by one, they were left with fewer clothes until they completely stripped off their rags. Then the stakes went up and it became a punishment.

They would have to give a very horny kiss to whoever was pointed out, and so the night went, between obscene laughter and a morbid atmosphere, which soon ended when the couples were chosen to have sex there, or where they liked to do it. No one stayed in the cabin where they celebrated the arrival of the New Year. Some couples accommodated themselves and others resolutely selected by the turn of luck in the bottle. They were leaving little by little the place that everyone had in mind. Oscar took his girl and they stopped at the first motel in the neighborhood they saw along the way. They finished drinking the bottle they had snatched from the party, put a porn channel on TV and together sexually enjoyed their bodies until they were exhausted. Already awake, together they bathed, boarded the car, and went to dinner at a restaurant in the city of Monterrey located just above Garza Sada Avenue. They ate, drank, commented on what happened the night before and said goodbye. A cheerful farewell with the memory of a crazy night.

Oscar worked as a lawyer and worked for a dispatch of a highly experienced and well-connected former police commander in the field of the tasks and obligations of the State and Federal Police, he had his flaws. His duty was to always be available, by cell phone or radio. Most of his co-workers were people with great expertise in matters of corruption, embezzlement, fraud, and knowledge of how to act in the perverse of a twisted and inconvenient justice. So, to relate to such people was to enter the field of arbitrariness, iniquity, and abuse and illicit.

The management of the firm's business was based on the permanent connection between the legal and the illegal. Between good and evil. It was about pursuing, monitoring, and extorting those who wanted to be stopped or apprehended, even if the persecuted were not the bad guys of a given event. I mean. The head of the firm received a confidential secret about a case to investigate and usually had to be caught by those responsible for the wrongdoing. But on many occasions, they went to the archives of the released or those who once purged a sentence in prison, and these were re-consigned with nothing to do with the problem in turn. It came to pass that when time was coming to them and it was urgent to present a solution to the case in question, because of the pressure that the authorities exerted, or because the media pressed on all fronts, they were in urgent need of catching any individual who walked down the street, and this individual was given all the law by putting him in jail, even if he pleaded not guilty. Like this case, many, including the same authorities, knew of the slander to which the individual was being subjected. And they crossed their arms. Divine justice!

Oscar, immersed in the realm of corrupted law, was imbued with that underground trap of the ruined lawyer, and constituted by the intrigue and deception. Sought an unhealthy image among others, projecting himself as a greedy being, seller of the word or exhibiting an infamous brat at truth and justice. A provocateur and trickster, an immoral, betraying his profession without an ethic to rule it. Far from being an honorable man, from being a good interpreter of law, far from having class to defend the values of equity, conscience, and expressions of a humanist spirit. Lost in a malicious work, perverted in an abysmal judgment of pride, away from honesty and righteousness, handling without modesty an unworthy sense of justice. The classic second-rate lawyer whose only duty was to do and execute exactly what his boss commanded him, and blindly obeyed his reactionary impulses.

Over the years Oscar had gained a lot of experience in all these needs. Lawyer, defender of the chief on duty, known for the environment in which he was developing and protected by a police badge that protected him. Well personally trained by his bosses and esteemed for his loyalty to the position, he was a perfect candidate to be selected in any case to be solved. Oscar over here and Oscar over there and giving strong results with the reality of the actions. Showing his badge everywhere.

As good as he was at speaking, he was equally good at using his fists. He would have been a splendid boxer in the ring. He had already knocked out some guys defending the integrity of his bosses in some bar and on the street, bypassing traffic. His fists were considered a white weapon. After each fight, he left his mark on the faces of his rivals. He did more damage than a street person, exchanging jabs with another individual. It was like a hammer-wielding weapon over the humanity of its opponent. He was a very good protector of his companions, shielding them. A fearless guy with extreme speed to move in altercations with other men of the same profession. His bosses also admired him for his unwrapping when it came to taking out the revolver.

Besides everything else, as a car driver he was extremely skilled and capable.

He had no competition in front of the wheel. Bold, fast, and brave. He had excellent resources to get around the traffic, even if he was driving on a very crowded street. Panic was non-existent on his face. A guy who was a little more than six feet tall, broad-shouldered, rough-handed and blood-expression. Crude to walk and talk. Thick lips and populated eyebrows. Direct with his expressions and robotic when receiving orders. An exemplary mold rolling in a medium turbulent, but perfect for the purposes of the profession...That's how Oscar was.

CHAPTER IX

Two weekends later Laura and Edgar toured the floors of the Presidents Museum. Unique in the country. Beautiful documentary exhibition. With valuable objects protected by safeguards, such as the presidential sash that was the first president in Mexico. But above all and most importantly, here they honored Don Venustiano Carranza. Some of his furniture, a military uniform and other belongings that are interesting when touring the enclosure is displayed. Carranza was born in the Coahuilense territory and is an undisputed reference in the Mexican Revolution. Edgar, while he was reading or explaining the imported paintings, suddenly dared to kiss Laura's cheeks. Some kind of stolen caress. He was very close behind her and he would spread his lips delicately. From there, they moved to the Desert Museum. A strategic building, built on a hill, allowing itself to be admired from afar. Another jewel of important value for the museum. An excellent excuse to spend a weekend accompanied by a partner and fully enjoy many objects, pictures, images, monoliths, scale specimens, dinosaur skeletons, Tyrannosaurus, and more. Whose remains, it is said, were found in

Coahuilense territory according to the annals of history. And so, walking through the corridors in half light, they took their hands and intertwined their fingers, as if they were sealing the joy of a pleasant afternoon.

They were vacated late from the museum and its knowledge. Then they both craved a succulent dinner and a nice glass of wine. Six o'clock hit and they were laughing, enjoying, and chatting about everything. Sharing notes, data, historical memories, geographical, and other doodles. Arriving to the car, Edgar intended to open the door for her, as a gentlemanly act. By chance of fate, her waist was trapped by his arm as she set out to invite her into the car. Their bodies came together so much that not kissing would have been more sinful than doing so. What happens if I kiss you? He asked her. Laura smiled in complicity to his desire. Edgar wrapped the minuscule size of Laura with his arms and asked her again. "What happens if I kiss you?" She also held him by contributing to his adventure. She showed an unnamed smile and deliberately drew her lips even closer. Waiting for the menacing kiss. Total silence. The sound of the engine of the trucks reigned, which perceived deaf in his ears. A second later, the prison of the warning kiss was lit like a fuse in the gunpowder, with great force and enthusiasm. Another kiss came and another, and another, until they found themselves in urgent need of taking air to recover from suffocation. They finally got in the car. And as soon as they did, the pilgrimage of their kisses continued without a truce. A long time without taking enough rest. The night began to rob its protagonism in the afternoon and the shadows darkened the panorama. Suddenly the lovers were surprised by an armed guard of a lamp who urged them to withdraw from the parking lot. The incident was both celebrated with great laughter. They looked at the watchman understanding his boldness. They had about an hour of kissing inside the car.

Forced by circumstances, Edgar innocently asked her where she preferred to be at that hour. "Which restaurant? Which bar? Give me an idea! Please cooperate." Astonished he was when he heard from her lips, preying on any objection that might arise at that instant.

"I want to be alone with you, in a place where no one looks at us and enjoy the way you will surely love me under four-walled prison."

Once again, she caught him, taking the lead.

Her prompt and unexpected response was like a slap in the face for him about his experience with women. So much so that Laura smiled at the face of complete perplexity. Indeed, he expected everything but this. Once again this "doll" grabbed the bull by the horns. Carrying the initiative. A woman who is ahead of the male proposal. I want to be alone with you! I mean, she didn't wait for the man's word, his point of view, his opinion. No! She was a female deciding where to be and with whom to be, right. Directly determined, without prejudice, to the grace of his authenticity. A female defending her context under the power of her word. She openly said, "I want to be alone with you!" It meant that she wanted to be with him because she wanted him and was not subject to the man's decision to be taken to bed. Because he was the one who asked where she would rather be at that hour? And she elatedly responded, "with you and alone". So, at that hour and with those premises, Edgar's erection and moisture in his body were logical in his spinal cord.

Edgar thought that this liberated reference from his companion, expressed a diaphanous voice, of a woman not conceived and detached from prejudices that society through all time imposed on women for decades, self-denying, subjected to their word. Tied to her man's powerful arm, supposedly to be protected. To him, Laura was a being outside of that old misogynistic context dragged for centuries in Mexico. Of course, he was happy with that desire, he was pleased to be liked by Laura. So, Edgar decided to take her to his house and not to a motel. To my house, yes sir. *I'll feel so much better to show you what's mine.* She deserved it. He was proud to meet a woman who had sanity and courage to choose from. A philosopher like the Spaniard, *Fernando Savater*, would have given him a good lesson regarding this situation.

As he said, he took her to his house. Domiciled almost on the outskirts of the city heading west of the state. Edgar lived in an exquisite neighborhood, unpopular, fractional, and somewhat removed from the great avenues. A two-story house that had a living room, a television, and a full kitchen. Upstairs he had disassembled a room and turned it into a library. And he had another room in case there was a need to receive any visitors. Among the rooms on the upper floor was an area that functioned as an anteroom in which Edgar heard his favorite records or watched a football match. Having shown his home, he suggested listening to music, having a drink, and dancing for a while. Laura raised her shoulders and said nothing. She got carried away by her partner who proved to be an excellent dancer. They heard soft, silky, slow music, suitable for the moment.

The bed greeted them at about nine o'clock at night. Without having tasted food. They didn't care. She ripped him off his long-sleeved plaid shirt and cowboy-like trousers, unbuttoned his wide belt with a large buckle. And He took off her all-white clothes. He admired with extreme sensuality her legs, well rounded and muscular. Unhurriedly, slowly, and comfortably, they hugged, kissed, and penetrated their bodies like two lovers who had already known each other. They both walked their eyes through their companion's entire body. He admired his *cinnamon toned doll*, and she adored her portentous tramp.

He rejoiced in the skin of his naked companion. Her cinnamon skin shined with the rays of the electric light; they made love with the lights on. When their sexual debate began, they didn't think about turning them off. He imagined that he made love with the beautiful Halle Berry in her most faithful film role of coquettishness. But when he saw her lose her hair bright, exuberant, black, combined with the curves of her waist and nipples imploring the bold kiss, he imagined being at the foot of the great Griffith Joyner, the Olympic super athlete of striking personality. His eyes bathed with a cascade of overflowing hair over his face. Tingling his nose. The fullness of her breasts, upright and gymnasts, were swinging over his beard rubbing with extreme passion. At the rate when her gray eyes crashed with his black eyes.

She, smiling, loving, willing, affectionate, dedicated, did not hide the fact that she was passionate about her lover's body. A woman who clearly liked her man's profile. The man she had in bed now. Because there are those who have sex but don't like their lover's body. And there are women who don't like the body of a man. But Laura enjoyed what she had with her. She had fought for it. She saw her companion now, joyful, excited, witty, surrendered, and slick. A man who didn't ask that he was ahead, being loved by a hardened lover.

While Edgar was distracted by something else in his mind. He never remembered ever being with a woman capable of being taken away with that desire, with those desires that ran over his inventive in love. As the men in the neighborhood say, a female, who participates, undertakes, and creates the envious journey to orgasm.

When the clock crossed the hands to midnight, she marveled at him again. She took her cell phone, called her house, and told her father without preamble that she was going to sleep with Edgar. Laura dictated her address where she was and provided him with Edgar's phone number so her father wouldn't worry. JJ thanked the gesture of her "little one." Making the call, the promise was born that the next morning everyone would have breakfast together. Edgar was astonished and left with his mouth open. He'd say alone, she left me stupid. Rarely does one learn that there are parents who know how to be friends with their children. He thought. And this is a pleasant example of which I am now a witness to. I like it. Another lady would have told a lie. Invented a tale of any kind, simulating scenes, quirky versions, despite the known discredit. Forcing me perhaps, to take her home in difficult hours of the morning. But no, everything was different than it was supposed to be. Although of course, Laura's age was enough of maturity, to have details of that magnitude. Anyway, he found her attitude very positive.

***

I lent them my night. The one that belonged to me, the passive and loving. The one you never see in a sea of violence. And in that peace, they didn't have to talk at times. Their love rested on a nest of promises, in a reserved source of dreams to be converted. Looking at each other to exchange finds and increase their connection of sounds. Debuting utterances and conjugating verbs. As it was supposed to be almost no sleep and when they had time to return to the talk, they talked about this and that, they stroked the unspeakable. Their lips looked like two erasers traveling all over the anatomy, swollen and red about to burst.

In the morning, they bathed together. The tub in the bathroom was greeted by smiling ones. They smiled with the soap that ran through their bodies at the same time. Later, they dressed and she very fresh, said:

"Hurry up, my parents are waiting for us for breakfast. Aren't you hungry? I'd eat a whole Canadian bear with everything including the salmon they swallow".

"Do we bring anything for breakfast? I wouldn't want to arrive empty-handed. Your parents will say I'm lazy".

"No problem. Mom made some stews so rich that you're going to suck your fingers. You'll see!"

They came home. Laura's parents welcomed Edgar as if he were already the family's political son. They sat him at the head of the table, right in front of her father. And just as it was New Year's, this time it was a shared, laughing table, dosed by good manners and with a clear example of parents who know how to educate their daughter who felt whole, lucid, and proud to communicate to them her joy of having found the man who has been waiting a long time. Laura, without any pity, commented that they had stayed at his house. They wouldn't have risked coming around town very late, it wasn't convenient. That's how Sunday took on the family's silhouette. Little Mariana took hold of Edgar's arm and did not leave him alone all day. He devoted himself patiently to storytelling to the girl, later the baby wanted to sleep on his chest and finally they took the car and together they all played ball in the gardens of the Urban Forest where they spent the rest of the afternoon. Returning, they visited a candy shop, tried several treats and Edgar, arriving to Laura's house, decided to return to his.

"Hey! Family," he said in a completely homely tone. "I'm leaving. I've had a great weekend.

Unforgettable. "He made his way to the yard where his parked car was waiting for him. This time, Laura and Edgar said goodbye with a prolonged kiss in front of the watch of Juan José and Layla. More than a romantic relationship had been born between them. For sure!

***

My city had turned a homeless man into a generous feeling. The look of my streets picked up the humility of a man polishing his thoughts. Rolling back and forth, back and forth, as Jose-Jose sang in his younger years as a singer, a man who, by the way, caused a larynx shattering prodigious voice. I'm sorry to invoke it, but I really liked the way he sang. That is why I affirm the sorrows perfect the profile of a man whose street experiences make him more human, wax his spirit among the many comings and goings of the shadows. So far, my insolence has scented the gravidity of a homeless man who has become an example of what I say. An insolent individual who has gone looking for a decent house, a wonderful lady waiting to be reciprocated. I wonder if he deserves it, having been locked up in jail and robbed money to survive. A thief who steals from a thief, right, but will he be exculpated in his conduct with that procedure? Just because, according to him, he acted sanely.

My city welcomed him with honors. Emerging out of nowhere now had a secure roof. From the empty one to the whole. Zero to a hundred. I like to say yes to things that have value. Satisfied I am when I can give something beyond simple company. I like my people to feel at home. Let them understand what's made up of one day, not just 24 hours. Let him bleed in the morning and come back safe and sound at night. May he be grateful to have given him a sun and a moon in so many hours? Here are these new lives that awaken a virtuous tomorrow. Loves that become promises of life. Families born from sneaky kisses. Here's to a future that started on a crazy night, for a crazy woman driving others crazy.

On the way home Edgar compared black and white. His fingers in relation to his hands. As always, comparisons are horrible, but it was worth it in this case to put them under the curtain. Rosario the woman he chased and could never have when he was in his thirties. The persecuted woman, the guarded woman, the longed-for. The one of the images suffered but loved by him to the unspeakable. The one who preferred to park her sentimental world next to someone else. That beautiful woman who at the altar was delivered by himself. He could never possess Rosario, as he possessed Laura today. He never felt like Rosario was his as he felt today to his combative brunette. And this princess was a woman-made goddess. A set of good things made just for him. This time he wasn't going to waste the gift that life had put in his hands. After the arouse circumstances, he reached the finish line.

It was Edgar's success to come and debut his wandering between my streets. No doubt. In a quiet, organized, planned and emblematic city. Here he found a woman from home. He even knew and didn't dislike the idea that he would have an adopted daughter. That's how he considered it. A flattering future in the hands of a family that welcomed him with good eyes. This was his destiny. There would be no more searches. He had come to his romantic lair.

Once with the sentimental issues put in place. He had rented a house on the shores of the city. Another hit. The question was how does someone value money that they're not supposed to have? Hidden money. Not inverted yet. It was like playing hide-and-seek. How to make an investment without putting on paper the name of the person who invests their capital in a transaction? Already very confident in the honorability of his partner, he thought to put his belongings in Laura's name. The house, the car, and any businesses he imagined in his plans. After all, he thought, her family had adopted him. That was a bigger hit.

This is how the figure of a homeless man comes to life within the sense of belonging. He is embedded among the living to live as a human and not as a ragged homeless man. Scum to all eyes. The bells of the church ring, to announce the arrival of a new pilgrim who was born among us.

***

Laura drew conclusions, three years had passed since she separated from that raw energumen. Today she restarted her sentimental life with a man made of another skin. Understanding, gentle, prepared, and much more human. She was fascinated by the respect he professed to her and the way he conducted himself.

After six months of establishing a serious relationship, their habits began to become customary. It was July. The routine of being with him had already occurred. Sometimes he would stay at home, but then Edgar would prefer to go to sleep at his. It made him laugh the day she invited him to sleep in her room. He opened his eyes as if he had been frightened and said, "were your parents here? Of course, silly, in my bedroom, you're not going to sleep with them. You're going to sleep with me, sweetie". "But what are they going to say? That I'm a gigolo sleeping in your bed". After the first night came the second and subsequent, with the passage of time he no longer paid much attention to those nocturnal details. From the last sixty days to date, it could be said that they lived together. Sleeping here or there was the same, although little by little her clothes and personal things began to move to her house. A fraction of a semester of dating had gained a lot of trust in both.

The security he felt in this romance prompted him to ask her, to please agree to put her name on the house that he had dreamed of to live in for the both of them. Three weeks earlier Edgar had arrived in a last model car with the title to her name. Now she was the one who was in shock. "Is it for me? but how?" "Well duh dummy, it can't be for Marianita, she still can't drive". "Please let me sell your *charchina*, give me the keys to your old car, almost useless, and thank it, at least, for the services provided over all these years. What do you think?" The sensational thing about this modality was that, with this new car, the five were going to be distracted on Sundays. Like a whole family.

To the movies, to the theater, to go eat or go to dinner or travel to Monterrey for a special walk. Edgar stopped being a stranger. The insubstantial tramp. That fortuitous visitor. Hye wasn't even considered Laura's pretenses. He was already an integral part of the family. Any planning included him, so that the parents when setting the table, would automatically think of the next dish as if he were their daughter's husband.

With the intimacy and the pillow, the grandparents assumed that at any time the couple would surprise them with a date to marry. No more, no less. They saw Edgar's arrival home with very good eyes. Her daughter Laura was happy, chatty, loving, accommodating. She improved her dealings with them, especially Marianita with whom she was now more tolerant. They noticed her patience and the way he drove to the neighborhood, taken by Edgar´s arm.

Although, her parents sometimes would overthink the idea of going beyond hypotheses and facing Edgar to ask him where he worked. What was he doing? What was he spending his time on? How would he make his money? But they did not dare because his daughter's suitor always behaved like a distinguished, well-spoken, very polite, excellently dressed, equitable and presentable man for all occasions. A man who treated their daughter wonderfully, to which he consented to surround her with loving details and advice. They even found out he had put his house under Lauras' name. Besides, he had bought her a car and regularly covered the bills every time they walked in and out of a restaurant.

He would frequently buy little Marianita clothes, toys, candy, or any bauble to keep her happy. I mean a better in-law wouldn't have been possible. Suddenly Juan José began to slide in some insinuations, but he went off the tangent saying that he had a store in the bank that paid him good dividends. He argued that he had small businesses that kept him busy on weekdays. Attending some small businesses of his in Saltillo and others in Monterrey so his time was really saturated.

Meanwhile, among the pleasant occupations of the grandparents, was to take their granddaughter to school. A small school located a little far from their home, they had decided to register her there because of the recommendations of the neighbors who had great reviews. Every day they dropped off the baby there and then often went to one of those American chain cafes where they tasted a cappuccino coffee in the company of a book in their hands. The two read their volume separately but very close together on the site. Layla loved to read esoteric books and biographies of illustrious characters, while JJ tasted Latin American literature. They kept the mania of collecting their books. Once they read the book, they signed it, put the date and place, and put it in the library, so that when they took it out of curiosity, they would realize where and when they had devoured their content. Detail that was never overlooked. And that same custom was digested by Laura. Her books were also autographed.

Anchored in such readings Juan Jose reviewed a few characters who were once also homeless. He remembered *Charles Chaplin* in his early film versions of the naive and sentimental homeless man who would give him worldwide fame. Also, by *Mario Moreno Cantinflas* who, working in circuses for years, became the most popular comical homeless man in Latin America. Or the shameless homeless *Tin–Tan* eating tacos on the streets of the city's slums. Perhaps, the unforgettable "School of Wanderers" that once starred Pedro Infante. And of course, he also had in his library the famous book of "Jack London" titled, *The Wanderers and Other Tales*. He could choose any of these characters to enrich his memory and move them clearly to the reality now lived by his daughter, in love with a flesh-and-blood wanderer, who overnight became an incredible and fantastic character cohabiting with his beloved daughter.

What did JJ as a father teach his beautiful daughter Laura to stand out from vulgarity? No doubt he had filled her with advice and warnings. Her father would say things to Laura like, "You must try to be independent". "Don't depend on the man". "When you live with a man, make sure you love and love him, because if you're with him just to feed you, you'll soon feel as empty as a glass without water around a served table". Her father had told her that; the woman must learn to be a woman, before making a life with a man.

"What do you mean, Dad?"

"That first you will have to learn to be you, to know yourself, and then to have the ability to love a man as your partner, without simply using it to possess his erection. Love is up to you, it's in you, not your partner. If you give love to whoever you want to give it to, you'll probably receive it back. But if you show your intention to cover an economic or maintenance need, the man with you will also feel the need to withstand the tensions between the two, until time says otherwise. However, it is very different to say;

"I love him because I need him, then to express, because I need him, I love him".

Despite these teachings, however, she was wrong about Oscar.

Laura was about to turn thirty-five. Everything was going well in her life, with her work, with her little Mariana, her parents as always together and the enthusiasm that was put into the love that surrounded her. Then Edgar would ask her, "Are you happy?" And she would respond with, "No, I'm not happy, I'm mega happy", smiling, saying it in a tone splattered with joy. Time had passed and Laura never wrote an article about worldly vagrancy. She didn't lack desire, but she didn't want to startle her partner. Several times he warned her that he did not want photographs, nor written reports with his name. Edgar fled from newspapers, from interviews by any reporter who approached him on the streets or at an event to get his opinion about a function. Laura would ask him, "until when are we going to have to live with the startle and he would answer, "I just don't know, all I know is that the moment they find out where I live and with whom, they'll send some thugs to kill me, and of course will hurt you, too. I'm sure of that. So, the less connected I am to the world, the better for me".

Suddenly Laura was attacked by bad feelings about the attitude of Mariana's biological father. She well knew that this guy was connected to the bad guys, with drug dealers, to the mafia and to gangs of kidnapping. He was the son of a bad life. She wanted to hide the romance that she had with Edgar at all costs from Oscar. The bad guy and the good guy. As a result, she knew that evil usually destroys well, and fear of impunity increases insecurity among Mexicans. There's a reason we're positioned as one of the most corrupt countries in the globe. So, she thought. Something good must come up. I trust it will. But then sometimes she thought about telling Edgar the possibility that they would both go to live in another part of the country. To another State of the Republic. Even going to live in the United States. Perhaps there they would live more peacefully and without the constant fear of being caught by the crooks, but she saw him so happy and loving that she dared not advise those things.

Both had become accustomed to their cuddles, smiles, jokes, compliments, and pick up lines. He liked sports. He was a supporter of all the teams wearing red. That's funny! The red in football, the red in soccer or in National or American baseball, which they broadcasted on television. Laura had fun listening to him screaming over a bad refereeing mark. Tremendous surprise caused the family when on one occasion he came home showing in-hand tickets to go to the football stadium to see a game between the *Rayados of Monterrey* against *Los Diablos Rojos del Toluca*. Obviously, everyone went. What fun they had.

They had a good time. But also, within the youthful environment they heard vulgarities and rude words that even Mariana never understood. Even Edgar had to explain the meaning of some vulgar expressions they were unaware of. Laura was calm and understanding with him. She liked to see him happy. That afternoon they ate tacos outside the stadium. It was quite an event.

Just on August 18, he invited Laura, on a date, to an Italian restaurant. The place where he first unmasked his personality. It was a rainy Saturday. The former homeless man waited for her at her house as he chatted with Don José about trivial *comsi, comsa* and unimportant things. Upon arrival at her house, Edgar kissed her as if she were already his wife, he hugged her and waited for her to get ready to leave. Don José accompanied them to Laura's car, said goodbye to both, and smiling as the couple left for the promised place.

In the restaurant, the talk was initiated and advanced by him. He had important things in mind and wanted to put them on the table as soon as possible:

"I'm glad we got a good table. Away from the door. I don't want to be interrupted by what I want to tell you.

She was bewildered, smiled, and asked candidly, while Edgar held her hands trapped between his own.

"Well, what do you propose?

"Ma'am, would you like me to be your chauffeur for the rest of your life?

Suddenly Laura didn't know what to answer. Because without insinuating it, Edgar made her a gigantic proposal, considering the substance of it. Well, that's what she thought, with the way he approached the matter, so Laura followed the game.

"It all depends. I'm picky, eh? I need a very disciplined chauffeur, precise, respectful, well dressed, and clean. Also, someone who doesn't let me go the other way when I tell him my fate every time I get in the car. And he must take care of me as much as if I were his property".

"There are many demands for your hiring, don't you think?"

"And I think they're the minimums that must exist between an employee and boss. Now, let me tell you something, we'll have to sign a contract, eh! Because just like this, no, ok!

At the end of the previous hiring conditions, she paused and added:

"Also, tell me what purpose would you pursue as you seek this job? In case you are chosen".

"I'd be fascinated to drive your persona all the time. Imagine being responsible for your life and the life of your child. Take you home, to your office, anywhere you choose to entertain yourself inside or outside in this big city, and mainly, open the door for you every time you get in and out of the car. I'd be honored. Although I must warn you. This chauffeur is jealous and requires exclusivity. Impossible to hire another chauffeur, ever again! I would be the only person authorized by you to always take you to a happy destination".

Edgar smiled, her face millimeters from his. And in that instant. From the inside pocket of his coat, he took out a small box and bloomed a ring that he tried to place immediately on one of her fingers.

"Tell me that I have just won the lottery! And that you have decided to be driven through the multiple paths by a homeless man in love with his future. Do you accept?"

She's been waiting for this for months. She thought he was never going to make up his mind. And today he did it in a totally unexpected way. What an irony she would have never imagined, as far as the ravages of that sad night flowed when her *charchina* broke down.

"Of course I accept, my dear tramp! Of course I do! Of course! I've spent the happiest months of my life with you. You've made my daughter, my parents happy, and I've been hypnotized. You're a polished diamond that has accidentally come into our lives. Being your wife will be like winning the jackpot in the lottery. I love you!"

Something she was pretty sure about. This delicate and gentle man was the diametrically opposite of Oscar. While this one was dreamy and romantic; the other from the beginning was possessive, clingy and totalitarian. Edgar was human and sensitive, and the other one was a hostile moron, he was like the thorns of a cactus.

That night Edgar left her at home. He didn't want to sleep in her room. He wanted to be alone and so he had told her. "Honey, is December okay for you to unite our lives? It will only be a matter of assigning the exact date of the wedding. What do you think? And we can celebrate this big commitment that will make us happy. Long live life! Don't you think?"

Immediately after anchoring herself at home, she quickly notified her parents with the news. Everyone celebrated it well and was beautiful. Laura told them the details of the statement. Beautiful, unusual, and original words. Her bum had laid wonders for her with his intentions. Being loved by that man had been a plan from that calendar. A globetrotter with his heart in his hand.

Layla took the glasses out of the display case and the three of them set out to toast and celebrate like grasshoppers the night when their daughter enjoyed the love of a bohemian, who officially became the man of her life. And together they began to plan what that ideal day would be to get married.

CHAPTER X

October dawned on its classic nights where the sun and moon stand exactly in relation to Earth. I mean, the terrestrials enjoy wonderful full moon nights. My city intercepted among the wounded, dead, and missing from present-day Mexico, the spiteful morning vapors with its trajectory. Nights weren't always made for love. Sometimes darkness is exploited as an anonymity of the popular good. Thousands of people are the ones who don't know the good, and before they have that fortune, they'll die. It's weird to say this, but it is. In this world there is black and white, and sometimes they cannot be mixed. The light and dark don't combine, only in the movies from ancient times. I'm not alarmed.

This reminds me of *The Godfather*. A fantastic novel brought to the cinema by *Mario Puzo*. An Italian in the United States. He created a true saga of films that came to my city beyond the eighties. Where *Marlon Brando's* figure plays and performs one of the best roles in his history as a film actor. The Godfather was a critical and commercial success, a tape exposing the dichotomy between two adjacent worlds. Coppola dared to bring to the cinema a complex story in an artistic way, where the action and horror were very intense and unique.

But going back to my city. My streets feature several monuments that can be admired. The imposing facade of the Athenaeum. The old walls of the *Escuela Normal* are for teachers. They are beautiful architectures, yes, very beautiful. Two reference paths in the education of young people, in addition to the immensity of its university. Although these are not enough to remove evil. It happens like in the United States. There are excellent schools with great teachers and yet one day a crazy guy arrives with a shotgun, broken from his brain sheltered by horrible thoughts, and he's about to shoot right-handed and sinister at his classmates inside the classroom. So, that stupid guy kills the first one he finds. Schools in the United States, held by these mentally deviants, are a serious example of the danger of evil, far exceeding the fringes of good. I wonder, why does evil prevail over good? I say this because today you can see that crime has overtaken my country. It is found and felt everywhere. You can even smell it, really.

***

Laura let the hot days of August and warm days of September go by. Now she expects October to cross fast over her schedule. She yearns for next December like never before. And it's because by then, her illusion would have formed. She smiled at the time of being a homeless man's girlfriend and later would become a chauffeur's wife. Contradictions of life. I gave myself to him to take me. I opened up for him to come in. I showed myself to get him to draw me. That's how I wanted to consume myself, in him. If I would have presented myself as idle, maybe he wouldn't have even found the gaze of my love. Avoiding your invitation, it would have been simple, but one thing I'm sure of. I am yours because I want to contrast with my old town, where the woman was usually chosen by the preferences of the male.

On Wednesday of the third week of October, like any other day, Laura arrived at the parking lot of the building where she worked. She sought out her space to park her car in, but on one side of the usual place she saw an unknown van, whose model and make did not have her importance. She parked her Jetta, turned off the engine and got out of the car still with the keys in her hand, ready to put the lock with the car's key control. In an instant and without waiting for, she received an impressive slap. Her car keys flew up. Her purse escaped from her arms. The bluntness of the hit was so certain that without any other direction, she went to the floor. Like a lump of cement in the middle of work. The stupor was high." What was going on? When only her mind tried to make things clear, the gorilla in front of her lifted her up as if she were a broom and raised her female corporeity to the level of his eyes. The guy who assaulted her looked like a swollen balloon. Laura, with her legs out of control and not touching the floor, was being imprisoned by Oscar who had her suspended in the air, without her being able to do anything about it. She immediately began to hear his claims...

"Do you think you'll get away with it? Fucking old bitch. What example are you setting for Mariana? A girl who ignores the lust of your sex nights with that piece of shit!"

Stunned and perplexed, kicking in the air, beaten and with her ex-husband's fetid breath in her mouth, she did not hesitate to answer, nor to defend herself. Her bewilderment was total because of the assault of the sudden offender. Still with the pain in her jaw, she could hardly attend to her assailant´s claims, who continued with the outrage by shaking her as hard as he could.

"I know very well who you're hanging out with, old prick. With a bearded guy and well-dressed, he's falling in love with you. Since when are you sleeping with that one? Answer me, you whore!"

Oscar kept her hanging and holding her from the white flaps of the jacket she was wearing that morning.

"I warn you. If I ever see you with that bastard on the street or inside your car again, the one who's going to pay for it is your family. You know well that I know your house, where you live next to your parents, I know where you work and where Mariana's school is. Believe me, I will do everything I can to make your life unhappy. So, you know stupid! If you don't leave that dumbass, I'll take it out on your family. You'll see!"

After saying everything he had in mind, Oscar threw Laura towards the door of her car but fell to the floor on her knees. And to top it off, he kicked her in the ass and spit at her that went straight to the target of her blouse. She was left like jelly on the ground, terrified, speechless in the face of the onslaught. Oscar got on his truck that was parked next to her, he ignited it and took off. Right now, she saw the reason for that strangely standing car in that place. Still, she heard clearly as the tires slipped on the parking lot pavement. In the end he escaped among the other levels of the great building. What a moment!

With effort and pain, she approached the elevator. She would have preferred to run home and tell her father what happened. But there were already many permissions requested from the head of her department, she was not going to leave her job just like that. So, Laura came to her office, closed the door, threw herself in her armchair and went hard into tears and sadness, as if she were a girl when she learnt that ghosts exist. As she stretched her arms on the desk, she noticed that her hands trembled uncontrolledly. She was shivering her teeth as if the cold in the office was ten below zero. She leaned her head in her arms resting on the desk. She vented. In that posture she remained about fifteen minutes. Fortunately, no one noticed her affliction. Soon after, she went over the scene of what happened. A monster possessed her person. This one wanted to stop her from re-ranging her life. He threatened her family and her little girl, the treasure of her days. Also, Oscar had every opportunity to win and nothing to impede the moment, mainly in the matter of surprise and brute force. But how can this be prevented from being repeated? How to stop this from taking the same audacity? Should she tell Edgar about what happened? Should she go to the police and report the outrage? In the complaint she would have to give names and details, in which was precisely the recommendation of Edgar who had long notified her. "Laura, I want to go unnoticed by the authorities," for fear of being located by the Prison Wolf.

Unable to concentrate fully on her labors she spent the day amid complaints, crying, and regrets. "Damn the time I married this bastard who continues to harass me despite the strict limitations imposed on him by the divorce clauses." When she gave the time, she left her office rapidly and uninterrupted. She wanted to come to her house and talk to her father, who was a man of regularly accurate, conscious appraisals. An old sea wolf, who knows everything about everyone. Arriving home, she took him to his room and effectively told him details, the sudden appearance of the monster in the parking lot, and the innumerable number of insults he lavished upon her, including of course, the abuse he put her through.

"Father of mine, I am very distressed. Extremely worried. What do I do to keep this wretched one from bothering me again? Besides, how did he know about Edgar?"

"Ah my child, it was easy for him! You know well he sees Marianita every month. Remember, he takes her for a whole weekend. Therefore, he has enough time to interrogate the girl and know what is going on in our house. And even more, you know that monster is constantly watching you. We've even caught him red-handed by following you through the streets of the city".

"What can I do to prevent this from happening to me again? Shall I tell lawyer Juan Carlos to re-file a complaint? I know the judge warned him that he couldn't get closer to me more than three hundred feet away. He's been violating that rule, dad. Not only does he chase me and watch me, but now he's got me threatened. What if I tell Edgar, Father?"

"I wouldn't advise that, huh?"

"Why?

"Surely Oscar would go looking for Edgar to face him and put two men who love you face-to-face. One for the good and the other on the path of violence. And as you and I know, Oscar would get away with the arrogance in which he rules his impulses, and because he's very well connected to evil people. That way I don't advise you!"

"Then what? Shall I keep quiet, wait for the next beating?"

"No! Neither my god. I advise you to call Juan Carlos and as a good lawyer, he will tell us what we can do about it. Let's hope this doesn't go unpunished as it is accustomed here in our country".

The afternoon of the next day they visited the lawyer's office. They brought him up to date with the events. Leaving nothing to the imagination of what had happened. They even commented on Laura's upcoming marriage plans with Edgar. Of course, she said nothing about the conditions of shelter, to which she was obliged to continue sheltering the surreptitious personality of her pretenses. She repeated to him how many times it was necessary, the intimidation that was caused by Oscar and how he attacked her that morning in the parking lot. The lawyer wanted to have as much information as possible, he didn't care for the moment, to investigate Laura's boyfriend. It was enough for him to know the details that the aggressor used to subdue her.

"Did anyone notice when that guy was assaulting you?" The lawyer inquired, hoping to find an eyewitness in the mishap. It would have been ideal to screw him like the last time.

"No one, unfortunately. Because the truck he was driving was high enough and big enough to cover up my car. So, he threw me to the ground between the cars. He certainly planned his assault very well," Laura said trying to provide more information to the case.

Juan Carlos, the lawyer concluded that he did not have enough information to file a complaint against the offender. He advised her to always bring a camera or cell phone on hand, to capture any time she deemed essential. He also suggested to always be accompanied anywhere. I think it would be wise for you to tell your partner, he told Laura, looking at her in the eye, trying to come after you every day. I guess Oscar knows where you work. The lawyer then turned to Laura's father and instructed that this would make it difficult for the assailant to hit his daughter again. Oh, and something else, Laura. If he tries to hit you again or at least approach you dangerously, immediately look for a military man, a soldier. Don't look for a uniformed cop. Today, as Mexico is, it's easy to find a military man on any corner. Go immediately to them and have them become witnesses to have evidence of his misdeed. Because otherwise, all we'll have is his word against ours. And we won't get anywhere this way. I'm telling you!

Having visited the lawyer, making things clear, made Laura satisfied with the step taken, and although they had not reached anything in particular, at least, she had now set a precedent going to inform a juris consultation of what happened.

"Father, if I ask Edgar to come for me every day, he's going to find it strange. Don't you think?"

"I don't think so! Your wedding day is coming. It is a good excuse to ask, in the appropriate tone, such a favor. If you see that things keep getting worse, we'll have no choice but to tell him what you're going through. For the time being, I agree with the lawyer. You must not walk anywhere by yourself. Even if Edgar can't, then I'll come for you to the office, as many times as necessary".

"What about my mom?"

"Don't worry, daughter, I'll tell her my way and without alarming her, about what is happening. I don't want to disturb her with assumptions or information that would only be at the level of our imagination.

***

Meanwhile Edgar was traveling in another galaxy. He looked happy. He had a very quiet time. The shadow of his past in prison was going further away. He wasn't so mortified anymore. The memory of the days living in prison was blurring with the good things that happened to him today. He used his time to fix his personal things before giving himself up completely to his new marital status. He was putting matters in place. Just like he wanted. The car he was driving was under Laura's name. In addition to the latest model car that he had given her days before with an invoice and registration sticker was also under her name. That is, Edgar had made enough arrangements in the cars and to liquidate the house where he currently lived at a low and convincing price. With the papers in hand, he had quickly put everything in the name of his fiancée. Of course, on the important date of the sale, she had to go sign. Not only that, but the furniture also he was acquiring in the same way came out under his girlfriend's name. His ebony soul resisted at first, but in the end, he convinced her, it was best for both. For Laura, the joy of participating in his things and owning his material goods, including his feelings, gave her a guarantee that this man was faithful to her, loyal and she considered him entirely her own.

Edgar hadn't spent a lot, not even half his riches. The money he still had left was hidden in his house. Incredible but true, kept it like grandmothers in the old days, under the mattress. When he bought the house, the first thing he did was to look for a bed. He bought a spring mattress being this, one of the most common types. These mattresses have an additional layer of comfort whose function allows an appropriate position of the spine. The money has been in there ever since. That double bottom served him perfectly for this purpose. So, he drilled the mattress, laid the stacks of bills, and sewed it again with extreme delicacy. Who would think of looking inside a mattress for an unsuspected amount of money? Living in the 21st century, no one. He conditioned his house in a such way that, upon entering, his wife would see a castle for her princess once the wedding was consummated.

By mutual agreement they had designated the second Saturday of December for the marriage liaison, a little before the beginning of winter. The honeymoon would be spent in *Las Cabañas de Monterreal*, just an hour's drive from the city. A dream place and exquisite taste, for a newly married couple. Anyway, the chosen paradise looked like a Canadian forest and was only within walking distance. A week and a half later, according to their plans they would be present to spend it together with the family and fully enjoy Christmas and New Year.

So, when Laura asked Edgar to go to the office every afternoon for her, the pediment seemed to him singular and romantic. "Why"? "Because I want everyone to see me with you! You'll be my husband. I have nothing to hide from anyone. And I would be very proud to introduce you to any coworker so that they meet the man who makes me happy."

"Besides, aren't you my chauffeur for life? Remember?"

"That's right! Smiling, he accepted his responsibility. I'm going to have to take a bath every day. Since you asked your chauffeur to always be clean and well dressed".

***

One of so many days, waiting for his fiancée inside his car, Edgar read a novel by *Jorge Ibargüengoitia* with the title *Estas ruinas que ves*. He read a story that was half nostalgic and half ironic. Painted within a totally provincial environment. Two years ago, he had already read to this author: *Los pasos de López,* and had marveled at him in the first instance, his spectacular way of telling a story only conceived in his imagination. It was the story of an independent hero discovered in his exponential inventiveness. A book to keep after reading, in the library. Occasionally, he would look up to see if Laura left the building where she worked. Located in a nice neighborhood. The city of Saltillo has improved a lot, he thought. It is no longer that big town surrounded by ranches and big estates that still dominated the seventies. Now its urbanization has had another face, very changed. Its bridges, uneven walkways, and its roads improved, the entrance to the city by Venustiano Carranza gave it an air of dignity, sober at the same time. A pride for those of us who live here. While he was in those considerations was when he noticed the latest model van that parked against the corner where he was waiting. It looked familiar to him. He had already seen it another afternoon parked in the same place. Not every day, but occasionally. It wasn't easy to forget a truck like that. It was a cream-colored Ford, with a closed rear cabin. The driver, always wore dark sunglasses and a tie, smoked impatiently, opened his window, and waited for someone. Edgar didn't know who. I think he lives very close to our home, he imagined, because he travels the same path as us. But then I lost track of him, a couple of streets before I got home.

While he was distracted with that, was when he saw his gray-eyed brunette come out of the building where she spent most of the day. As always, she was lucid and adorned with white as spring, white as the dove of peace and white he felt her penetrate the car.

"Hello, my love, how was your day today. Is everything fine?"

That's what he asked her, while giving her a welcome kiss when she got into the car.

"Yes, very well, everything in order. You know, moving forward with things that go out day by day. Preparing subheadings, reports, interviews, and news that should be embedded as they arrive. In addition to advertising ads to consider placing in tomorrow's edition. But it's all right. The good thing is that I already know how the advertising business is handled on our pages and that makes my task easier."

Laura also noticed the infamous van, only she knew who was driving it and what he was there for, unfortunately. He was the bodyguard of a police chief in Monterrey, but he would drive around to keep an eye on her. Waiting for her to get out of her job. What distress. Being harassed all the time as if she were a despicable criminal. This prick behind us, intimidating us with his constant appearances. Getting on my nerves all the time. He escorts us with apparent peace of mind, but I know, things could change in a dizzying way at any moment.

Autumn came, peeking out of a fresh November, and the spying had not ceased. Laura was distracted by the activities of the wedding preparations. She wanted a simple ceremony. She had discussed it with her father and separately with her future spouse. The simpler and less expensive the wedding, the better. A quiet civil ceremony, with a few guests, only the necessary and indispensable; and a discreet toast where there were no scandals or noises outside. Everything calm. Edgar loved this proposal; he thought it was wonderful. Zero fuss. Well planned. The whole event was at home. No orchestra, no raucous music, no rented venue, no ads in the paper. A humble and prudence-induced home. Of course, it was concomitant with Edgar's pretensions. Everything would go as planned.

***

Oscar had received a subpoena requiring his presence in order to clarify a complaint against him. Juan Carlos knew perfectly well that this was not going to even give him a headache. However, what he sought was to put him on notice through this recourse. Make him aware that they were unwilling to tolerate what happened in the parking lot again. The aforementioned was presented on the required date. He was told that in recent days he had been violating the marked disposition, in relation to the distance he should keep towards Laura. But because the lawsuit was not well-founded by the lack of eyewitnesses or photographs proving the facts, Oscar easily freed himself from the mess.

Wounded again in his ego, Oscar, receded over his line of fire that he wished to keep with his ex-wife. He wasn't going to take his finger off the line.

Everything seemed very suspicious to him. The damn guy who would follow Laura every day, wouldn't leave her. Edgar and Laura would go out everywhere together and behave like husband and wife. The follower felt there was something else they were hiding and urged him to learn how that stupid bearded man of fine glasses ruled Laura. So, he had no doubts about sending an emissary of his trust and remaining outside his home night and day. Of course, according to him, well disguised to avoid being discovered. Who was going to suspect a car washer or a uniformed guard guarding the corner house?

Fifteen days later the detective reported his work to the boss, informing him about the situation. He then learned that that famous bearded man lived with her. Then he took her and brought her home from her job and drove the car all the way. And on weekends the whole family went to the Alameda, downtown or the cinema accompanied by the bearded man. Or for a walk in the mountain range. He even took photographs of how his daughter Mariana would hold on to that strange man's arms. But there was something else. He had surprised them twice, going to San Pedro Garza García, to the neighboring State of Nuevo León, to visit a very prestigious house of dresses for brides, where they designed the bridal sets. So the detective assumed they were both about to get married.

Hearing the entire version collected by his trusted emissary, Oscar was overwhelmed with immensely great sorrow. A set of feelings, jealousy, resentment, anger, and helplessness. True, three years had passed since his separation, but he was still watching the steps of what had been his wife. Then he remembered his promise. "As long as I'm not happy with another woman, she shouldn't be happy with another man either." Pain with pain is paid for. But today with this news that reached his throat, it drowned him with anger. He was unaware of who Laura's new partner was, but he would end any project they had in mind. He'd find out every detail of his personality. Oscar was urged to know who he was about to face.

CHAPTER XI

On the last days of November, I began to receive the cold fronts of the season. The icy temperature is sometimes impertinent and disturbs the bones of my inhabitants. The thermometer runs on scales that with disrespectful consistency, range below zero Celsius. That's when my streetscapes take on a different hue. Looks like London. It gets so cloudy in the mornings that sometimes the mist in its foolishness persists after noon. In the peripheral the cars transit more slowly. The streets and avenues take a London photograph. Massive crashes of up to thirty cars are caused by the fog so thick that it is felt. The cold gets into the marrow. The homeless know the bitterness of the snowfall and seek quick shelter. Not necessarily under the bridges as John the tramp did.

On a Wednesday afternoon, Edgar decides to make a stop before arriving to pick up Laura. He drives along Francisco Coss Avenue and gets into the supermarket's parking lot, right in front of the city's large library. Parks his vehicle in any stall and goes to make the purchases he has in mind. He wants to surprise Laura by buying her some cookies that she loves to savor. They're her favorites at breakfast time.

And he'll also take the opportunity to buy himself a bottle of red wine. He likes to drink it regularly, from drink to drink, a bottle of Cabernet Sauvignon. It's a bitter drink, but warm and tasty when it glides through the palate.

Edgar took about an hour. Looking at the shelves and picking out the goods. He made the purchases, paid in the corresponding box, and left the store bound for his car that he looked for. "I left it here, didn't I?" He thought quietly. Walked a little further. "Did I leave it around here? Nope. Where did I leave it?" Toured the huge parking lot looking for his car without any luck. He spends a long hour trying to find it until he gives up. Then he calls Laura on a cell phone, who is surprised that he hasn't come to her like every day. Obviously, she wants to know about his whereabouts.

"Love! An unforeseen event. Looks like I won't be able to pick you up. I can't find the car, I'm sure it was stolen from me. I've been looking for it for a while and nothing."

"Where are you?" She asks him quite uneasily.

"I came to the supermarket. I parked by Francisco Coss Avenue in front of the Main Library."

Edgar feels the urgent need to go file a report of the theft of his car, to prevent someone from using it later for another purpose."

"Please Laura, call a taxi and go home. I'll arrive later as soon as I get out of this. Do you want to? I have to report the car theft to the authorities. It's very important."

"You could do it tomorrow, Edgar. Don't do it today, it's too late. Please come pick me up. It's already starting to get dark; I'm scared."

Laura was trying to prevent them from walking the streets alone. Something could happen to the both of them. She knew full well that she was threatened, monitored, including him, but she didn't want her partner to find out yet.

"Love! Take it easy, will you? I'm sure my car was stolen. I have to go report the robbery to the appropriate authorities. I can't leave it like that. Understand! The car can be used for something illegal. You know how things are handled today."

"It's all right! Be careful, let me know where you are to catch up to you in a while. sounds good?"

"All right, I'll call you from where I'm from. Bye."

After talking to Laura, he checks his watch, it was six-thirty in the afternoon, and he decides to take one last look. The learned route put him back on guard. Walked back to the left and then to the right without having the fortune of finding his *charchina*. He then heads to the taxi place on the corner, in which he is intercepted by a uniformed policeman, approached, and asked kindly:

"Hey, buddy? Did you lose something? I noticed that you have gone around the parking lot several times," the policeman said graciously, trying to be friendly.

"Yes! I parked my car here and I can't seem to find it. A lover of the other people's things took it away."

"And what was your car like? Any special details?"

"It's a light blue 2013 Ford model. I'm in a hurry to go file the complaint because I don't want my car used to rob or assault someone. Things aren't right these days at all."

"Well, if you want, I'll take you to the police station to make the complaint. I'm on duty, that's what I'm here for, boss. What do you think?"

The policeman told him that his police car was a few steps away and to please follow him. But Edgar, distrustful and feeling insecure, didn't accept.

"Thank you very much, really," Edgar replied respectfully, "I'd rather take one more look and see if I can accomplish anything."

Despite the refusals, the policeman did not give up and insisted that it was best to go and report it immediately. He confirmed to Edgar what he feared so much, "stolen cars are often used to steal or assault, to kidnap a person, to rob a bank or even to kill and run away. I recommend you end up reporting it to the cop to report the theft of your vehicle to the police station, right now."

The officer behaved so insistently, he sometimes seemed foolish and stubborn. He followed him to where he was walking. He would look for his face and with his hands made a great effort in the air to be convincing.

Well, I think it'll be best, Edgar thought to do what this gentleman says, right now. He finally agreed to get in the police car. He let himself be driven by the kind uniformed. They reached the official vehicle, and he invited him to sit in the front seat. behind, there was another policeman inside, who from the inside greeted him affable with a half-false smile.

As a passenger on a police car, he trusted the policemen to drive through the streets. Meanwhile, they distracted him by talking about this and that the driver was going down the avenues very quickly. He would turn rapidly and then go beyond the streets, until they encountered a dead-end street, car free. To his astonishment, the car turned to the right, went through an open gate, and transited a second later a gravel road. At the end of the site to what looked like an unused parking lot, three guys were waiting for them, among them stood out a tall, muscular man with a generous abdomen and rough face like a displeasured person. He was wearing a suit and tie. The car continued to advance and stopped until the passenger's door was within his reach. The man in the suit opened the passenger's door and pulled Edgar by the hair until he was dragged to the floor. Once again, the surprise that Oscar would put in his actions was an advantage, for any individual who wanted to defend himself. Punching was his favorite weapon. Of course, Edgar didn't expect it. In a matter of moments, they beat him between the four guys, without mercy. Edgar imagined that eventually the Prison Wolf had found him. He felt that in seconds they would end his existence. He decided to defend himself as far as his strength allowed him to. Although neither were willing to leave him alone. By majority, four against one, he was easy prey to his opponents.

Oscar, the guy with the tie, put all his effort into beating him up. Another cop held him by the jacket while the rest of the uniformed had him held tight from behind. There was no escape. One pulled his hair back. Another with his legs wrapped around his, holding him and the last guy had him secured from the belt.

"Here you're going to die, motherfucker," Oscar said furiously.

"Why are you beating me, why, what did I do to you?" Edgar shouted, desperate, completely confused.

Because that brunette girl you've been cuddling with, is mine. Just for that, asshole.

He grabbed him by the testicles and squeezed them tight enough to bend him instantly.

"Do you understand, you fucking bastard? You're going to die right now!"

The beating revived the screams of the man with the suit and tie in the face of the victim. Some were up and others below, but within a few minutes they had him as a punching bag. As Edgar could, he tried to pull the gun out of the belt of a cop who had tripped, but right then he was hit with the pipe that was held by the man with the tie. He broke his skull. From that moment Edgar no longer felt anything, he bit the dust, but unconscious. Throughout all that, they kept kicking him in the face like they wanted to disfigure his face, until they got tired. Edgar's right leg was tailored for Oscar's rage, to take out his outrage. He broke his knee. Visibly Edgar looked dead.

Seconds later, they all searched his pockets. His cell phone, watch, wallet, and ID were ripped off.

Voter's license and credentials were sufficient. Oscar wanted to find out who this bearded asshole was that with Laura, his ex-wife. He didn't throw anything away. He kept everything. He carefully put them inside the pocket of his coat. He'd then check them carefully.

Edgar totally annihilated, was out of combat. He didn't notice the rest anymore. In his condition he looked like a corpse. Oscar ordered the uniformed cops to throw the dead man over by the apple trees behind the *Sierra de Arteaga*. The cops changed vehicles and grabbed another truck with the bed of the trunk covered. They wrapped the body with a large tarp, picked him up and turned on the vehicle. That's where the job ended. With the credentials on hand, Oscar assured how much they would help him to investigate who this filthy man was that intended to be the suitor of his daughter's mother.

***

Nine o'clock at night and Edgar hadn't called back. Laura found it very strange not to hear from him when he was known to be in contact with her almost every hour. He also told her that the car had been stolen precisely in those days when everything was complicated. She called him several times on his cell phone and nothing, she was sent to the voice mailbox each time.

The temperature got colder by then. At eleven-thirty at night, they decided to go look for him. Where? Who knows, but they weren't going to stand there waiting for divine providence to perform a miracle for them. What they were looking for was outside. That's how it was. Don José told Layla to stay with the girl and wait at home. The first one who had any news would make it known to everyone else. Both father and daughter left headed to the large parking lot where Edgar said his car had been stolen. The supermarket by then was closed. Everything was darkness and the parking lots looked empty, with one car parked, like scattered cells at night. They had been looking for someone that could help. Any young man who used to be there to help drivers park their vehicle, or those kids who take care of washing them while the owner does their shopping. But nothing. The place at that hour, in the cold, didn't lend itself to people walking around.

It then occurred to them to go to the police station to see if Edgar had reported the car theft, but nothing was reported. Inclusively, they didn't have any reports about any stolen cars in that area. With the refusal on their forehead but determination, they immediately went to the Red Cross Hospital. They arrived and they asked at the reception desk if they had seen a man with Edgar's peculiar characteristics, but they were still unlucky to have any information. They didn't find him. Heartbroken they got in the car and inside Laura broke into tears. Her father didn't know what to do or tell her. What advice does someone give their daughter when her man whom she loved so much, close to marrying, had mysteriously disappeared?

"Daughter, what if your suitor decided to run and escape your presence?"

She saw him with baffled eyes and her father responded quickly...

"I'm just assuming daughter, for God's sake! Don't look at me like that!"

She stayed silent. She thought about it, but she didn't want to get the idea that he did. She remembered him entirely, with his words, with his caresses, and when they would make love. He was so intense and loving that it was hard to imagine what her father had aforesaid.

The clock hit three-thirty in the morning. Saddened, they exchanged assumptions and opinions to get an idea of where Edgar might be at that time. They had the last resort left, go to his house. He could be there, maybe he got sick and decided not to bother anyone, taking haven in his house. Let's go! Said the father cheering on his daughter.

They took the whole freeway close to the exit of *Torreón*. They turned right towards the Saltillo 2000 area, a fairly clean popular neighborhood. Minutes later they arrived at his house. Laura had the keys. That, that house was already owned by her, with that in mind that her fiancé wanted nothing under his name. She had not gone to that house for almost two months. They entered, and their first surprise was that the house seemed to be completely disused. The refrigerator door was open, probably because there was no food inside, so Edgar kept it that way, to prevent its interior from creating bad smells. There were her personal things, she recognized them. But the house was changed from the last time she was there. Edgar had ordered to manufacture an integrated kitchen with mahogany wood and his white table, it looked beautiful. She contemplated for a moment. As she climbed up, Laura noticed the freshly made closets with the sober taste of someone who likes to live well and, with discreet luxury. In the main bedroom he had installed a huge painting where she was the protagonist. And next to the head of the bed was the picture of his newlywed parents. A photograph where JJ and Layla posed more than 30 years ago. Surely the photograph had been secretly obtained from her belongings. Seeing all this, Laura bursted into tears, but this time with greater force. There were tears, screams, and immense pain that Laura felt. Don José was forced to help her. Laura's father thought during that moment that his next son-in-law possessed true sentimental values. He really loved his daughter, showing him all the details. He adorned his house for the sole purpose of giving his fiancée the pleasure and security of feeling loved by him. JJ would never doubt Edgar again.

After a while they went down to the living room. Laura made her dad a coffee and called her mother to give her bad news. Sitting in the armchairs, they talked about her fiancé's details. A well conducted man, with all this, was about to confess to her father her boyfriend's tortuous past, but she felt that it was not yet time to do so. Surprisingly her cell phone rang, she pulled it out of her purse and the screen announced Edgar's name. It's him! She yelled at her father; he's calling! Her face lit up, looking at the cell phone screen. She put her finger on the screen and took the device to her ear; but she listened only to the noise of a car engine. Hello! Hello! And no one answered. Until she shouted; are you there, Edgar?

Answer me, please! Edgar! But she never heard his voice. Until the tone of the so-called ghost was lost.

***

Fifteen days passed and there was nothing to be known about Edgar. They had been present at the police station to report his missing. Not only Edgar's, but also the car that he drove. They revisited the Red Cross leaving there two advertisements placed on the walls. They also went to the DIF, (National Integral System for the Development of the Family), to the bus station, even Don José came up with the banal idea of going to the morgue. Any effort, they thought, might be wise to find him.

Suddenly, one morning Laura came to mind the idea of visiting the editor-in-chief who runs the "security section" in the editorials of the newspaper where she worked at and told him about her misery with details. The confession sensitized him and promised to be on the slope in case he knew anything about it. Besides, he told her, I've got a very insightful reporter on the list in that regard. He has a lot of ability to zigzag through the information of such thefts, mainly from cars. I'll keep you posted.

This unusual action soon paid off. Within days the reporter entrusted knew of the discovery of an abandoned car in the vicinity of the municipal dump, with the signs previously pointed out. Plates, vehicle model, color, and general conditions. They immediately went to the junk yard. Laura and her father realized the condition of the car. They found no papers of any kind. Neither the registration information nor his license, but they found in the trunk one of his jackets. She took it into her hands as if it was the only oasis in the desert.

With an abnormal passion in her daughter's tone, she told her father with real vehemence.

"Edgar didn't escape, Dad. He didn't go anywhere. His car is here with this jacket. We went to his house, and it was intact. We found no indication that he wanted to pack. Prove he didn't run away, as you assumed. Someone did something to him. You and I know, and very well, the imbecile man who did this to him."

She laid on her father's chest and began to cry. Her weeping spread for hours and hours without finding comfort in her sadness.

"They killed my man, Dad. And this bastard sent people to kill him, Dad!"

Don José didn't say anything anymore, he knew Laura was right. The only one who could have committed such a felony was within reach.

Laura, infuriated, didn't know which way to take to appease her grudges and do justice. Her son of a bitch ex-husband had beaten her this time, only she was waiting for the final news. Normally, so was her married life beside her daughter's father; he beat her almost since the first time they met, giving her a dog's life, always threatening her, never ending his night parties, misunderstood Mariana, but very lively with street whores, and finally, this. Make the man she planned to remake her life with disappear. At that moment she thought; if he did anything to Edgar, he's going to pay for it with his life.

***

In a crude room, that is, without polished walls, built of brick, without windows, with a concrete roof and unpainted, they went to throw Edgar's body, beyond the direction of *San Antonio de las Alazanas*. A small village of nearly a thousand inhabitants. Far behind the large areas of apple trees, near the mountainous slopes, where not a single person arrives, it is an almost wild wilderness territory. Way over there, they went to dump the stripping of his body. The uniformed cops thought that, from the beating he received, this guy was more than dead. In fact, they couldn't hear his breathing. The bloody lump wrapped in a tarp, they tossed him inside the room and set out to return.

Edgar was unconscious for a day and a half. When he went back to reality as soon as he woke up, he realized that he was in a place that horribly reeked of excrement. It was night when he awakened. He couldn't see anything. He knew it because a very dim light was peeking out on the floor. He approached this ray of light and was able to make sure it was an illuminated corner where the height of a metal door culminated. Chest to ground he proved that it was. It was all darkness; he couldn't see anything beyond. The most cautious thing to do was to wait for daylight and see the possibility of receiving help from someone.

When the first rays of the day announced the sunrise, his illuminated power did not cross the threshold of the metal door where he was locked. So, the clarity was insufficient before his eyes. With all that, he checked the condition of his wounds. His fingers recognized the clotted blood on his face. One scab on the forehead, one near the back of the head. He thought he had a hole in his skull because his middle finger was sinking somewhat in relation to the circumference of his head. One eye still hurt quite a bit. He could swear that, in front of the mirror, he was red. He had it closed, swollen. He couldn't move his shoulder very well, the jabs of pain didn't leave him alone, and he claimed to have it dislocated. His legs had wounds at knee level. But his right leg exhibited exposed fractures, his tibia and fibula, which Edgar treated with great care, because only poking the part caused immense pain. It haunted him to be able to kneel nor lean with his arms. He was practically immovable. it was impossible to try to stand up. All this suffering reminded him of the beating received by the "wolf" and his allies, in the years when he was in prison. Although the affliction now wasn't very different. At first, he thought that was the reason for the assault, but now he remembered that the guy in the suit was screaming in his ear with all his might, "because that brunette girl you've been cuddling with, is mine, asshole". He reflected then that the motive for the altercation was another. He knew no other brunette woman but Laura, and if that was really the problem, a matter of jealousy or sentimental order,

Laura's silence would have been mortally damaging. Because he wasn't aware of anything about it.

The sun jumped above the mountains, but in the brick-built room, with no windows, it was only perceived by a slit as tiny as a shadow on a rainy day. He spent hours lying on the floor waiting for someone to stop by to help, but not nothing. He could hear the truck engine in the distance. He estimated that maybe they were at a distance of about five or six kilometers, maybe longer. He didn't hear the natural bustle of a population. No people screaming. He didn't expect anyone to go through the place where he was confined as a corpse.

On the early morning of the second day, he noticed someone scratching the door. The day wasn't cleared yet, it would be around half past five. A boar had probably sniffed it and came to see if he could find anything to eat. In the afternoon, a tremendous downpour fell that blessed him, because the fragile construction featured leaks, which became fresh spouts and he was able to drink rainwater as he pleased, it was a gift from the sky. And while he didn't quite distinguish it, he assumed it was water falling from the clouds, because everything was failing him, except his ear.

On the third day, the enclosure and rottenness of the place made him cry. He sensed that the room smelled worse, and his body was beginning to emit unpleasant smells. He noticed smells similar to human waste. As the days went by, Edgar's extreme weakness caught the attention of the animals in the mountains. At night, some wolves appeared that approached snooping under the door. But because they could not reach their prey, they gave up and left.

On the fifth day he began to faint. The wounds were infected at the point of rot, he didn't want to scratch. Itching caused irritations that turned into pus. And although the exposed bones of the fracture were covered with his jacket, he knew that the venom would advance unmercifully. Abandoned to his misfortune, he seemed to be impersonating *"Job"*. The good, covered with evil. Huge pain through this adversity, perhaps without a return. Satan is subduing me. He's testing the integrity of my fidelity. But I will not renounce Him, and I know that even at the last moment, He could come to my rescue. I, who now has enough money hidden in the mattress, a house of my own, a car and love with whom to enjoy it with, see myself in misery. Although I would get rid of them in exchange for forgiveness. "Another example of evil beating the righteous." "I don't break, no." "And in these miserable conditions I continue to ask God to have mercy on me."

Six days later and hurt everywhere, unsalted, without the essential services to live and in brutal solitude, he was accountable to himself. Hungry and thirsty, he lost weight fast. In such circumstances, panic was already roaming Edgar's mind. Abandonment and cruel isolation haunted him. He suffered the logical consequence of famine. He was slowly dying from starvation. In his lucid lapses, he had flashbacks about his motives. He spoke aloud to himself, as if exercising his conscience: "I'm sorry, I'm really sorry Laura." I wanted to live what you gave me.

I enjoyed your company, your body and your space. Thank you, thank you so much for loving me the way that I have always wanted to be loved". But without wishing it, he would remember his captor's infamous phrase, with his qualifier, "because she is mine, asshole!". What was Laura hiding from me that this guy hates me so much? Was it her ex-husband on a macabre plan? Or a guy who she had an affair with? Why didn't she ever tell me anything? Why?

Ten days later, Edgar was incredibly alive and among his vomits ended up defeating him. Imminence to the afterlife awaited him irretrievably. A ray of light accomplice to a rainy storm showed a small portion in the corner of the corner, against his body, several bones of human skeletons. The vision no longer frightened him, he assumed that this cursed place was the morgue of what they call, "the disappeared." That's how he would end up. Converted into a skeleton. He confirmed that this filthy hut was a cemetery and that's where the wretched cops had gone to throw him away.

Nights and days were passing through his eyes and the faint light no longer made a dent in his sanity. He let time run. He didn't mind collecting unpayable debts anymore. He was his worst enemy in these conditions. At times, his lucidity allowed him to say goodbye to his memories. Mainly from his Laura, despite the terrible uncertainty in which she left him. In other times, time had been his best companion, even in his thicket, even today, he thanked it. The filthy, creepy hut away from the population and orphaned among the undergrowth of the mountain was certainly useful for uniformed thugs. A site for human remains, perfect place to make selected individuals disappear. Would he be the only one? Of course, not? Surely there would be more places like this. That's how the underworld police work. It was a matter of luck to fall into anyone. He didn't know if the night would come or if it would leave. He fell asleep in the bone dump where he was planted. Without being able to cope with his misery and body weakness, he disappeared from the sensory world, until his senses ceased to be noticeable.

***

Meanwhile, during those days, Oscar entertained himself with several tasks in his office, including investigating the credentials that he had taken from Edgar. Calling here and there, checking files, searching the internet, making other calls and unique issues that modernity now possesses, to find the identity of the one he had already considered dead. He found out he was an ex-con still wanted by the same prison authorities, where he had served his sentence. His departure from the penalty was classified as a suspect as his defense attorney argued for actions outside of legal context, in order to achieve his probation. In the quest for more information Oscar also learned that a gang of drug traffickers was after his whereabouts. They claimed to have let him get away with a very large amount of money.

Once Oscar found out about all this, he was almost certain that Laura didn´t know what kind of person she had been entangled with. Oscar sensed that this ex-con, traced by law, was hiding under the veil of another personality. Even if his official credentials said otherwise. Anyway, it would be a matter of putting his finger on the wound and informing his ex-wife when the occasion would present itself. But how would he get to her, because the moment he would do it, he would be giving himself away. On the other hand, he knew Edgar was already in another world. Evidently, he sensed that his ex would guess he was the killer.

***

Consciousness and time. Traits dependent on the fear factor that propelled the machinery of his thoughts. Laura apprehensive and frivolous. Laura reflective and introspective. Laura submerged in the chronology of the last events of her missing Edgar. In the order of her ideas and with the temperament she possessed, it was impossible to imagine that she would be resigned to the infamous episodes. She could not be eternalized waiting for the arrival of her man, when she almost confirmed that he was dead. And despite planning and rethinking again of where to go and what to do, in the face of the overturned disappearance of his lover, to surrender was not an option. The useless wait had reached the roof. Something had to be done and soon. She argued that her fiancé had fallen into Oscar's hands. But what to do? Where to go? How do you force him to open his mouth and confess his crime? She even thought about getting a gun and going to kill him.

She, knowing where Oscar worked, asked her father and lawyer Juan Carlos to accompany her to that wretched man's office, and see if she could get information from him with the whereabouts of her beloved Edgar. She managed to get a reporter with everything and a camera to achieve the greatest possible impact. Agreeing on the time, they met on the streets of downtown Monterrey. They left the vehicles parked to the attached building where they were meeting and arrived at the law firm where Oscar worked.

His office was located on the third level. When opening the elevator, she went directly to the fairly extensive display window where the receptionist did her day-to-day work, assembled with a computer and a couple of telephone extensions. Passing the reception opened a rectangular office in which the lawyers of the Head of the firm were placed side by side, with their respective desks. At the core of this space was a fairly elegant door, covered with walnut wood, which closed, was supposed to have access to the CEO President.

Very determined, the four of them made it to the third floor and started rolling the plan. The reporter carried the camera on his shoulder with his respective credentials on his chest, the lawyer wore his best suit and Don José wore a suit, tie, and a hat, and carried a good-sized cell phone in his hand, just in case. Without respecting the "stop" announced to them by the receptionist, they walked straight to the adjoining office that Laura had ever visited when she was Oscar's wife. She already knew the way. Laura opened the glass door and went straight to her ex's desk for questioning.

Laura was immediately intercepted by Oscar's gaze. She was almost running towards him, her lips cracked, sealed and with hatred in her eyes capable of tearing down a building. His astonishment was enormous, he did not know what to do at the time. Oscar would always punch people; it was his favorite weapon because he would disarm and knock out the opponent. But now he was the one who was stunned and received the unexpected visit in a shocking way from his ex, who arrived with a truly explosive attitude, causing the general bewilderment of the office. Just as he was trying to put away Edgar's credentials of whose identity he was looking into.

"I want you to tell me, right now! What did you do with this gentleman?"

At the same time, she showed him an amplified, colored photograph. Oscar then saw that she was accompanied by a rather nourished entourage, because they surrounded him immediately. The reporter's camera was right on his face. He turned everywhere and nowhere in particular, showing his nervousness. He fell into the ambush and today he was the prey. He bit his lips and answered as best as he could.

"I don't know that person."

"What do you mean, you don't know him, you son of a bitch! If you threatened me weeks ago telling me that if you saw me with him, I was going to pay

— 211 —

dearly with my family. Did you not say that? Yes or no! You fat lard!"

Each sentence displayed placed greater emphasis and loudness. So, her voice began to spread all throughout the floor where they were.

"Where is he? Answer me you stupid fuck!"

"I told you ma'am; I don't know that gentleman!"

He wanted, with that expression, to completely depersonalize himself from the embarrassing situation.

Formulated that declaration that Laura found out of place. It gave her so much courage that, without thinking, she went over to Oscar's face with her claws out. She tore the skin of his face from the forehead to his chin, reaching for his fledgling goatee beard that had grown. Her fingernails brought Oscar's skin between her fingers. Apparently, she had already taken his measure. They were living in a moment to a similar situation as when they were married, only this time Oscar could not lay his hands on her. Wounded, he screamed too. He took his hands to his face to cover himself of what Laura had done to him with a grudge. In the impulse, she moved towards him in search of his face, Oscar pushed and tilted the desk and from its surface, fell a series of papers, letters, envelopes, and other documents. Among them, Laura distinguished Edgar's identity card as well as his driver's license. Immediately she picked them up from the floor and lifted them, shouted at him with all the courage she had on her.

"You don't know him, huh? What is this? You fat lard! I want you to tell me where he is. What did you do with him?"

Laura showed the credentials in the air for everyone in general to realize that Oscar knew her boyfriend's whereabouts. The scandal was major when the desk broke down where they were both fighting as gladiators to sustain their reason.

The reporter didn't lose detail with his camera, filming everything. And the others supported the chorus of screams that she emitted with the strength that remained to her. The riot took the office's CEO out of the office, and he realized what happened. Oscar was on the floor bleeding and four people surrounded him with a desire to gun him down.

"What's going on here?" The president shouted.

"It just so happens," with Laura's lawyer taking the lead, "that this individual," pointing him out with his index, "kidnapped or has this gentleman missing", showing Edgar's photograph. "As soon as we leave this place, we will go to the office of the Commander to file a lawsuit that you employ your underlings to kidnap and disappear innocent people. And believe me, it's going to be all over the papers tomorrow!"

The president of the firm, very well presented, observed the reporter with the camera that was filming him at that moment, turning towards him. The president was stunned. Motionless and frozen. At that moment, Laura returned to the attack.

"From here I'm heading to file a complaint against you," she said furiously, accusing you of hurting this person. I caught you red-handed. And it's on tape. You can't deny that you don't know him since you had his credentials in your possession. You know his whereabouts! And you'll have to answer that. You Bastard!"

"And you, Mr. President.," said the lawyer who faithfully accompanied Laura looking at the face of the CEO of the firm, "you will have to answer to the authorities, why you employ criminals among your trusted staff. Oh! and might as well tell you now, everything that has happened here and, in this moment, will be on television tonight."

Furthermore, with complete impudence and ensuring for everyone to see it, Don José, in turn, had taken photographs of all the events that occurred at the time. The office, Oscar's face, the credentials on his desk, the president's face, and the whole environment of the situation.

They quickly left the office after all that made magnum of screams, shouts, assertions, accusations and so on. And certainly, they went to the office of the Commander to report the events that to their satisfaction led to Oscar's bewilderment that, in all that period of the altercation, he failed to say something coherent.

"With the rod you measure, you will be measured", says a Bible verse.

CHAPTER XII

Two months passed and there wasn't any important news about Edgar's disappearance. Oscar was fired from the office and with the news that he was missing. Surely jobless, living at the expense of multiple deceptions and extortion, bad handling that came out perfectly. Fugitive from justice, because they were looking for him to clarify the whereabouts of Edgar and other disappearances. The accusation was filed, but he never showed up and the law was supposed to be after him.

Laura went countless times to ask about the progress of Edgar's search and to ask if they had caught her criminal ex-husband, but they always came up with the same preach. "We have not taken our eyes off your case, ma'am! Believe us. We're still watching, we haven't had any encouraging news. Unfortunately, there's nothing that leads us to having anything conclusive about that matter, but keep coming back ma'am, maybe one of these days, something will come up that gives us a clue. At least one sign."

JJ sensed, very cunningly, that the case was filed. Mostly if the wanted one was a fraternal friend of the uniformed. One more example of the impunity used in Mexico. Laura's father still remembered when he was little, that his parents entrusted him to a uniform, for him to protect. They'd tell him, "If you get lost, if you're missing something, or anyone wants to hurt you, go to a uniformed cop, we're sure they'll help you." Unthinkable to do that today! The cop in a blue or brown suit is now a symbol of corruption, perversion, and dishonesty. Thief or murderer. All mortals know that. It's in the public domain.

In a way Laura had resigned herself. Many nights and days she mourned her defunct suitor. How little it had lasted for her to taste! She had been passionate about a different man, distinguished, intelligent, studied, prepared, and aware of the needs of a woman like her and more than anything, with enough and capable wisdom to give love to her life. Time passed and the truth is that she had already given herself the idea of her ultimate disappearance. The imbecile of Oscar had killed him. She didn't know how, but she was sure he had done it. What a coincidence, he first threatens me in the parking lot, then they steal Edgar's car, then his credentials appear on his desk and then his untimely escape from the office where he worked, running away to not face justice. Of course he was involved! And from her head, no one was able to change her mind. Marianita's father had killed the love of her life.

"Mom! Why isn't Edgar coming anymore? I miss him. I want to see him."

"Me too daughter, I would like to see him, but it will no longer be possible. He went too far. And the most serious thing about all this is that I don't know what course he took."

Impossible to tell her child everything that had happened. And tell her that her father murdered Edgar. Impossible to detail to her what Edgar really was before he came into their lives. Impossible to tell her little Mariana every night she spent longing for him, dreaming of him, wanting to see him, to appear again to brighten her existence. Unfortunately, that was no longer possible. Edgar had disappeared from their lives overnight without warning. On weekends, they were no longer the same as for a year they were in his presence, who enlivened the talks with his philosophical or historical interventions, contradictory yes, but which provoked interesting conversations. A fine and special touch on the table. Today, on the other hand, at lunchtime, there were other topics surrounding the talks. On the table, on a daily basis was a constant complaint of the times lived. "Did you know they killed some boys around here and some other gentlemen over there?" "Hey, did you see the kidnappings of the actors who went on TV?" Kidnapping has already become an entire industry. Some people live on it. "Did I tell you, Mother, that the neighbor was assaulted on the road to Monterrey?" Every day here in our city, they implement the Code Red, it has become customary. What about the authorities? Where are they? Fine, thank you! It is increasingly noticeable how people are losing respect for our institutions. Doesn't the government realize that, or are they dumb? Jesus! What country we live in!

Edgar was gone. Oscar had fled and was no longer seeing his daughter every month. The days showed another reality. Work in the office, Mariana's school, which she now attended elementary school, with a different address. School supplies had to be purchased for the new student and she was tasked with reviewing her assignments. On Sundays they walked on Boulevard Carranza on those walks that were organized by the municipality. The walks were nice, and the family was better off walking under the morning sun. Her parents were aging, and she had no desire to continue, if anything, it was because of her baby, whom she donated the title of mother to. She was going to work because she had to, but not because something would give her the illusion of showing up.

Is it true that time heals everything? Bullshit. Time is a pilgrim companion to our misfortunes. When you say it, it has already passed. Time is never your friend, not even your confidant. It's that somebody you can't trust, because it runs, even if you wanted to stop it. It is impossible to tell the world to stop its movement of rotation and translation. It's impossible. Life is time and it goes away.

***

One afternoon after many when it's boring to go out on the street. Laura had worked two more hours of her normal schedule for arrears in publications that were due to appear the next morning. As she was leaving her office, the lights in the street were illuminating. She was just about to go home. An April, disproportionate, sad, without encouragement, announced the death of a day that had brought no news. She reached her car parked in the basement of the building and to her misfortune did not ignite. She spoke to her father and told him that she would take a taxi because her car, which Edgar had certainly given her, did not start. He no longer lived to repair her *charchina*.

Laura returned and went to the company's reception and ordered her coworker to please call a taxi for her, she didn't have something to leave in. When the taxi arrived, she went to the front door, peeked out, and turned left and right and vice versa several times. She didn't see anything weird, not even Oscar's truck, which she really would have found strange. She ignored the reason why, but she kept the memory of the old concern she sensed when Oscar mounted on the steering wheel of his van and watched her outside her office. Months had passed without sorrow or glory, after that heinous grievance, yet she kept the dabbing fear that caused her pain within her every time she thought of it. But well, time took care of erasing it, and today things had a different present. Ten minutes later the taxi made its appearance. The driver honked the horn, she got in the taxi and left. The driver prepared the taxi meter and the meter announced that he was ready to take off. He drove through the first seven streets without difficulty, took Abasolo Avenue and went down the slope to peek into the distance the peripheral of Luis Echeverría. In that corner they had to stop. The traffic light announced a red light. The driver waited for the green light to go. He turned on the radio with barely noticeable volume and played tropical music, pretty amusing. Laura took the opportunity to call her father, telling him in great detail what happened in a few words. She was sitting to the left of the rear seat distracted by the traffic jam, right behind the driver. During the call, she told her father that she would arrive soon, that she was already inside the taxi. Finishing her call, the phone went back inside her purse.

Effectively, she extended her gaze through the windshield. She noticed a cream-colored van in front of her that prevented her from seeing beyond. Laura couldn't distinguish very well; the night was getting heavy. Suddenly the traffic light announced green. But something weird was happening because the car in front of them wasn't moving forward. The taxi driver was unable to move. He honked the horn several times so that the car in front of him would move, but he was ignored. Then the driver grabbed the gear stick and reversed, turning around he realized that there was another van behind them, very close to his taxi. It wasn't moving either. They were trapped. The scene surprised them. The strange thing was that only these three cars were stranded on the avenue. The rest had left and disappeared. Laura got nervous, started sweating copiously all over her body. Her hands were shaking. She turned around at the same time as the taxi driver did, back and forth. Nothing, the cab was imprisoned. Impossible to move.

In that moment, Laura looked closely at the van in front that had them trapped, and she realizes that it is a bulky vehicle, without glass in the back. She also noticed that it didn't have license plates, she only saw the back of the truck, but Laura recalls the color from the day Oscar hit her inside the parking lot that morning. She put all her senses into remembering and ended in a matter of seconds admitting that effectively, it was that's the van Oscar was driving that day.

To her surprise, someone who she was unable to see the face of was standing right in front of the window where she was sitting. However, she was only able to see the abdomen, the man wore a tie and black coat. Her first impulse was to open the door, but the man standing by her window prevented her. She started screaming as loud as she could, the taxi driver got scared and wanted to get out of the car, but he thought about it too late. A guy standing in front of the cab points out a gun and at that moment the taxi driver gets shot between the eyes, he died instantly. The driver's blood splashes Laura's face who is about to faint. From her throat springs a frantic cry, she knows she's going to be killed, she's next.

Edgar, her father, her mother, her daughter, all these faces come to her mind, in a fraction of a second. Panic arises. Death haunts her. She sensed it ever since she exposed him in his office and the news of his aggressive visit came out in every newspaper in Monterrey and Saltillo. That's where he ended his career as a crook with a credential. She senses that in another second, she will also be killed. She suddenly feels that it'll be best if it happens. Disappearing like a lot of people have disappeared. A routine that has been happening in her beloved Mexico. Living in a country where everything disappears. Where impunity reigns.

She resigns herself, knowing that in the next moment, death will arise from wherever she is and say: "it is your turn".

Indeed, a couple of seconds after her dizzying rumination, Oscar appears with a gun in hand. His abdomen is no longer a curtain and exposes his cracked face—, because of the injuries that Laura caused that afternoon when she assaulted him in his office —, He reveals himself entirely behind the passenger's door, behind the annihilated taxi driver. With panic in her eyes, she contemplates the gun that Oscar is holding in his hand. She thought "it's my turn". Oscar, as tough as ever, opens the door on the side where she is sitting and...

"Why did you have to go report me? Why did you do that?" He yelled at her with glossy but resolute eyes, with his hand on the revolver. Those were the last words she heard. Laura knew that the appearance of her ex-husband was death in person, so she expelled without fright, everything she had stored in her chest.

"Because you have always, until now, been a murderer! I know I'm not the first, and I won't be the last. Cops like you do that. Go on! Shoot me! What's stopping you? Don't pity me, I'll still hate you in this lifetime and in the next one. You'll never change, you were born an animal, and you'll die being an animal. Completely irrational! Damn the time I found you! You fat fuck."

And without waiting any longer, Oscar pulled the trigger of his revolver...

***

Darkness reigns in my streets. The clock announces eight-thirty at night. The luminaires on the avenue are dim and the profile of the people are lost with the scattered brightness of almost all molten spotlights. The municipality regularly takes time to replenish them when there's an opportunity. It's always the same. It's a prevailing evil. I complain about the conditions in which they keep my streets and avenues. They leave everything until the end. At that time with the cold sensation in the streets, few dared to wander between the pavements of the sidewalks.

Oscar maneuvers his truck with extreme speed down Abasolo and driving straight until he reaches the freeway. He's crying and lamenting deeply for what he just did. He screams and cries, like a kid who just had his ice cream removed from his mouth. It was necessary to do it! He says himself... She left me no choice! He continues to drive his truck at full speed down the ups and downs of the fast roads until he reaches the highway to Monterrey. He looks for a convenient space and parks his heavy truck there. He turns to the adjoining seat where the wires he took from his ex-wife's Jetta are. He shuts down the engine and unleashes his pain. He gets out, vomits, coughs and cries biting his feelings. He's murdered what was once his soulmate. The woman he adored with all his heart and who couldn't give her what she was looking for.

When she told him. "Go on! Shoot me!" Irrational! "You were born an animal and you will die being an animal." "Damn the time I found you." "You fat fuck!" The deep hatred that Laura had for him hit his heart. He noticed the immense contempt that her eyes exhibited. He understood that it was totally repulsive to her. He realized that even if he lived a hundred years, he would never be able to master the temperament of this woman who once gave herself to him with such enthusiasm and fervor. With her gray eyes, with her angelic bronze body, her beautiful athletic legs and the small waist that supported her breasts like those of a young woman.

Without thinking too much Oscar had shot her in the forehead. Right between the eyes. Laura didn't even have time to close them. The arrival of death did not give him time to forgive, nor reflect, nor even a request that dying people get to have on their deathbed. She died suddenly. She then didn't say any words to offend him. He was done with the woman who marked his life. A dark-skinned woman did, but bestowed a white happiness, unattainable.

***

Being an urban spirit, I cannot hide and simulate the pain that exists in my people. It's a constant sense of helplessness. Affliction that is commented on in any corner. Death roams my streets, fears are disguised, people walk with their hands in their pockets, submissive, like religious people about to be crucified. Good and evil subsist as an employee and boss in the workshop, where flavors and unflavored are stored. The streets, no matter the time, are a minefield. In the corner, the silence breaks because a gang lurks and commits a heist in a convenience store. Halfway through the street, a full-speed driver runs over a passerby who had the nerve to cross his path. On another surrounding avenue, an adult is assaulted by a guy who carries a butcher knife, as big as a machete. He strips off his wallet and his credit cards. He couldn't stand the impression and the old man dies from a heart attack in that moment. Someone very skilled from a computer commits a millionaire fraud. Sadly, the fraudster will never be apprehended. An unscrupulous person will board an urban bus and with a gun in hand, will threaten passengers. He'll take money, jewelry, and cell phones. Fear will dampen the intimacies of passengers.

I question myself. If the killers ever wonder, where am I? What am I doing with my acquaintance's life? I'm sure they don't even know it themselves! They only act under an irrational instinct. It's no wonder that witnessing these barbarities in my city, Edgar and Laura have disappeared, in a world that will soon disappear because their own inhabitants will take care of it little by little.

Time continued, as always, unstoppable. Juan José and Layla mourned their daughter for many months, until leaving her memory in the cup of coffee. Little Mariana was left without parents. Her mother was dead, and her father wasn't there either, but if he was, she'd never see him again. The funeral, burial, and condolences resisted thanks to the presence of their beloved little granddaughter.

The Grandparents sought everywhere for a sensible answer, and obviously, also for the culprit of their daughter's murder. They clung to it, but they never obtained a clear answer. As usual, the police authorities behaved without going straight to the point, totally indolent, with vague preambles, with short and loose clauses, desert deviations, circumlocution, and extensive parentheses. Difficult to find a chronological order to the investigations and inquiries, and without reaching the backbone of the murder. Representatives of the law strayed over and over again in inaccuracies and made-up comments.

Therefore, the grandparents, after many months, finally gave up on the case, even knowing, who had been the killer. They never found the slightest hint of Oscar. Impunity killed him.

***

Since the calendar is an essential accessory and cannot be betrayed by marking dates and commemorations lightly, it is how we find what was left of the family, traveling in my city, heading home after having made some Christmas purchases. The night had already begun to get sad. But time doesn't care if someone is missing or if there is an extra person. It simply complies with the calendar and irretrievably marks the days to come. The thing is, it was December again, period. JJ drove his car with his Moroccan wife next to him, and his granddaughter entertained with the bows and wrappers in the backseat. Suddenly the Jetta they inherited from Laura, began to fail them and began to release smoke from the inside of the hood. JJ wanted to hurry up and get home with that car malfunction and although the dashboard warned him that his attention was urgent, his male foolishness pushed him to keep trying to reach his house.

But he didn't get very far, he had to move to the shoulder of the road, otherwise he was going to be in the middle of a busy road and that would have been a lot more embarrassing.

He got out of the car, lifted the hood of the car, the fumes coming out of the engine flooded his body. He moved from the front of his car and headed to Layla to tell her about the situation, while the radiator vapors scattered through the air. When he stood in the front of the car again, he crouched down and looked for the causes of the damage. He grabbed his cell phone and tried to locate a mechanic or friend to help him, but with his insistence he was unsuccessful. He called one and called another, but with his bad luck, he was unable to contact any of them. Despair began to make him sweat. In that moment, he caught a glimpse from the edge of his eyes, a shadow of an approaching individual. He was a homeless man who walked with severe amble, with ostensible limp, advancing pitifully supported by a stick as a cane. He exhibited a marked face, scarred, mucky, with snarled hair which reached his neck. With a somewhat gray beard, his eyes very sunken and a frank lunatic expression. When he reached his presence, the homeless man asked him with some candidness...

"Sir, may I help you with your *charchina*?"

JJ looked at him slowly, frightened, but scrutinizing. From head to toe. Astonished by the

emitted expression of the homeless. This man carried a light brown jacket, ripped from his elbows and lapels. A torn shirt that peeked out disobediently below his waist, and filthy ripped pants presenting his knees. Without much thought, and looking at him directly into his eyes, he asked him extremely intrigued...
"Who are you?"

If you are interested in sharing your comments with the author, please email him at:
romel1947@hotmail.com